To Karen
Remember your creator
Ecc. 12:1-6
        Danny Parton

Remember

GARY M. PARHAM

Remember

a novel

Tate Publishing *& Enterprises*

Remember
Copyright © 2011 by Gary M. Parham. All rights reserved.

No part of this publication may be reproduced, stored in a retrieval system or transmitted in any way by any means, electronic, mechanical, photocopy, recording or otherwise without the prior permission of the author except as provided by USA copyright law.

The opinions expressed by the author are not necessarily those of Tate Publishing, LLC.

Published by Tate Publishing & Enterprises, LLC
127 E. Trade Center Terrace | Mustang, Oklahoma 73064 USA
1.888.361.9473 | www.tatepublishing.com

Tate Publishing is committed to excellence in the publishing industry. The company reflects the philosophy established by the founders, based on Psalm 68:11,
"The Lord gave the word and great was the company of those who published it."

Book design copyright © 2011 by Tate Publishing, LLC. All rights reserved.
Cover design by Kenna Davis
Interior design by Christina Hicks

Published in the United States of America

ISBN: 978-1-61777-722-6
1. Fiction / Christian / Classic & Allegory
2. Fiction / Christian / General
11.07.15

ACKNOWLEDGMENTS

I can only start by acknowledging God for all He has done for me. Had He not saved me from my sin, I wouldn't have had anything to write about. He truly has put a new song in my heart!

Next to God is my wife, Karen, who has worked so hard helping me to write this book. She helped me with typing, grammar, and most of all, she encouraged me when I wanted to give up. I love you!

Also my children, Luke and Jake, who put up with me being locked away in my room night after night, week after week and never complained! Thank you, you both are such a blessing, and I am very proud of all you have accomplished in your few years on this earth. Most of all, I'm proud that you are living for Jesus!

I also want to thank those who have helped me with editing and publishing, Phil Hovey, Jennifer Minigh, and Debra Peppers. Thank you so much for your expertise!

TABLE OF CONTENTS

FOREWORD	9
PREFACE	11
THE KINGDOM	13
THREE ARE CHOSEN	18
THE BLEMISH	26
IN HIS IMAGE	33
THE FALL	37
SEEDS ARE SOWN	43
THE KINGDOM DIVIDED	49
A HAVEN	59
A STRANGE CREATURE	67
DECEIVED	74
THE CONSEQUENCE	79
DARKNESS SPREADS	88
NO OTHER WAY	95
AN UNEXPECTED VISITOR	105
LOVE TRIUMPHS	114
A SAFE RETURN	127
JUBIL'S REVENGE	134
A BIG MISTAKE	141
THE FINAL BATTLE	150

FOREWORD

Gary Parham has created a phenomenal God-inspired book that, in my opinion, parallels the works of C.S. Lewis. The reader is virtually unable to close one chapter without peeking ahead at the next. The descriptive language and amazing portrayals of both the antagonist and protagonist are riveting. All ages will be able to vividly visualize this account of creation, the fall, and man's glorious restoration. Gary Parham surreptitiously intertwines cloaked scripture with dialogue, while the reader is brought to peeks of emotion seeing their own life portrayed between the lines. I highly recommend this book for all ages and backgrounds, and especially those who would love to see God's sovereign plan creatively and beautifully come to life!

—Dr. Debra Peppers, National Teacher's Hall of Fame, University Instructor, Radio and Television Host

Great communicators take things that are complex and make them simple. Gary Parham has taken the greatest story ever told and has broken it down to a level that a child can understand. *Remember*, is a story of a king who had everything, except a family, and was willing to give up everything to have one. This book will inspire you, teach you, and build your faith, but most of all it gives you a glimpse of the heart of God that will change your life. Get ready to go on an adventure. You will journey through lands that will impact your soul and spirit as you experience God's compassion, grace, and understand His strategies for keeping you close. Gary has been in ministry for years. As his pastor, I have witnessed his walk with God firsthand. His personal testimony has given him the credentials for writing this exciting story about the journey of faith. You will be blessed as you pick up a book that you cannot put down.

—Pastor Bryan Cutshall, Twin Rivers Worship Center,
St. Louis, Missouri

Remember is a story that will cut through the soul of any reader. A story written between the lines of the Bible, it presents the Gospel in a fresh and creative way, yet stays right on the mark. In a world blinded with religiosity, the story of *Remember* will open the mind's eye to the big picture of life. This beautiful book has a simple storyline that can be taken to great depths, depending on the reader, and will unlock the door to conversations about truth, actions, and consequences. What dwells in the belly of *Remember* is the spirit of evangelism—otherwise known as the heart of Gary Parham. This book is an incredible evangelism tool that crosses the line of children's literature. It offers an unpretentious story that is not corrupted with false preconceptions of religion. Sometimes it's easier to lead folks to Jesus with a simple story instead of a five-point salvation plan, and this book presents an innovative prospect. Perhaps the way to the adult heart is to appeal to the inner child. In Matthew 18:3, Jesus gave us the real truth. He said, "I tell you the truth, unless you change and become like little children, you will never enter the kingdom of heaven" (NIV). Is it, then, a foolish notion that a children's book could have such a profound effect on the salvation of the world? I think not! Gary is certainly on to something here.

—Jennifer Minigh, PhD Biomedical Science, Author

PREFACE

The Bible says in Matthew 24:14 that the message of the kingdom will be preached to the entire world before the end comes. Today, we hear many messages; few are about the kingdom. We hear messages about prosperity, healing, and all the blessings that God has promised us while living on this earth. This is definitely good news to the believer. Even so, these blessings are still only temporal. In the end, all that really matters is where we will spend eternity. In fact, if we could keep our eyes more focused on the eternal than the temporal, life would be much richer. How awesome it is to know in our hearts that no matter what trial or tribulation we encounter in this life, we will spend eternity walking down streets of gold and living in a mansion built for us—to realize upon entering eternity, every believer, both family and friends that have gone before us, will greet us that day, knowing every tear will be wiped away, every sorrow lifted and joy will flood our hearts forever more. These are the greatest gifts God can give!

You see, I wrote this book because of a message God gave me one day while sharing Jesus with a man I met on a job. (I am a plumber by trade.) As I talked to him about Jesus, the Holy Spirit gave me a story about a King. This King went to a foreign land, leaving His riches behind, to find a family. There were many in His kingdom that He could have considered family, but they always knew Him in light of who He really was. The King desired family, but if they chose Him in the light, their motives might have been swayed by His riches and not simply by their love for Him. The King decided that the only way He could find a true family would be to go away to a foreign land disguised as a commoner. He would offer His kingdom to anyone who believed by faith, and those who received Him blindly would become His true family.

When He arrived, many mocked and rejected Him. The King pleaded with them and told them He only wanted to give them His kingdom. Finally, one person believed Him by faith and received great riches beyond his wildest imagination. After sharing this story, I looked at this man and said, "Can't you see that God has come here in the flesh and is asking us to receive His kingdom? Can't you see that God is not trying to take something from us; He is trying to give something to us? He wants to give us His kingdom!" I looked at the man and simply said, "Will you receive His kingdom?"

The man looked at me, and I saw life appear in his eyes. His whole countenance changed as these words came out of his mouth. "I would be a fool not to!"

That day, this man received Jesus as Lord and Savior. Years of religion became simplified through one little story. He could finally see the simple truth that God has created us to be His children. I believe this is why God asked me to write this book, so we could see the simplicity of the Gospel, the Good News of the kingdom. God created you and loves you. He put you here for one reason, to find your way back to Him. This world has become darkened, and this darkness has hidden God from us. Jesus, who was God in the flesh, has paid the price for that darkness and has become the door and the light for us to find our way back to Him, our way back home.

Some ask, "Is this life just a big test?"

I say, "Maybe it is. Maybe God has put us in a place where we can't see Him, only to find out if we will truly seek Him! Remember, if you love Him in darkness, then surely, you will love Him in light!"

THE KINGDOM

"I remember!" said Luke.

"Remember what?" spouted Jake.

"I remember the King. I remember our King. It's all coming back to me now. Somehow, I remember His name. I can see His face and the kingdom where we once lived. It's all right here in this book I found."

Jake, confused by Luke's words, asked, "What book?"

Luke looked up, and holding out an old, dark, dusty book replied, "This book; it's called *The Book of Remembrance*."

"Where did you find that old thing?" asked Jake.

"I found it up in the attic. I was up there cleaning and noticed it lying dusty and dirty tucked away in a corner, as if it was purposely placed there, and yet I don't remember owning it."

It was another dark and dreary day. Clouds had covered the light of the sun for many years now. The two brothers sat reading the book, enthused, yet somewhat befuddled by its words. As they continued to read, one brother's eyes were widening with excitement, while the other's remained narrowed, for though his interest was stirred, confusion dominated his mind.

He was wondering what could possibly be in this book to cause his brother to say such outlandish things? Was this book magic? Did it hold some special power? The book didn't look like much. It was old and filthy, much like the world in which they lived, a world where beauty, color, peace, and joy were a fading memory—a place where murmuring and complaining replaced a smile and a nod, sickness and disease took the place of long life, fighting and warring were the only sounds, and the smell of death was as common as the smell of fresh spring flowers had once been. It was a horrible and wicked world where the thoughts of men were evil all the time. You see, it all began many years ago in a kingdom far away, before the rebellion and before darkness spread like a blanket over the land. In this kingdom, everything was good, and all was well, until one day when everything changed. Who would have known that one choice could have caused such anarchy?

• • • • • • • • • • •

It was a bright and beautiful morning when King Adonai stepped out of His palace to look over His vast kingdom, which spanned as far as the eye could see. The sky was a bright turquoise blue, like that of the sea, with a large yellow sun that stood tall like a gigantic sunflower beaming down its warm rays of light. A few white, fluffy clouds formed into shapes for the King to gaze upon as they slowly drifted through the sky. Grass covered the ground like a thick, emerald green carpet, and each blade leaned toward the King as He walked along the path. Bordering the horizon were flowing golden fields with gently sloping hills, sprinkled with flowers of vivid colors, each filled with a sweet fragrance. Like the grass, the flowers turned their faces to the King so He could see their beauty. The trees that edged the field were like giant watchmen standing at attention, spreading their long branches toward the sky. As the gentle breeze blew, their branches swayed up and then slowly back down, as if in worship to the King. Running through the middle of the meadow was a river of living water, clear as crystal, which originated from the King's throne room, extending throughout His kingdom. As the waters flowed, the sound of a thousand voices praising His name resounded. All of this pleased the King.

Everything in this kingdom was vibrant and full of life; nothing ever aged or died. If the grass was stepped on, it would spring back to attention. The flowers always bloomed, and the birds sang continuously. The trees grew large, but they never grew old. They did not rot or die, nor did their limbs break off and fall to the ground. The leaves never withered, and the fruit never spoiled. No matter how long it hung on the tree, it was always perfectly ripe and ready to eat. The kingdom itself declared the greatness of its King. Even the sea would clap its waves in praise, and the very rocks would cry out to Him.

The King was very fond of the animals of the forest, the birds that filled the air, and the creatures of the sea. He talked with them while on His stroll to the city and called each one by name, even the tiniest sparrow was not overlooked. Up in the distance, the King noticed a young lion crouching behind an unsuspecting lamb that was grazing in the field. The King chuckled as the lion lunged forward and tackled the lamb, and they both rolled playfully in the grass. This is how it was in His kingdom. The lion lay with the lamb, the deer grazed with the wolves; everyone lived in harmony, creating a true paradise for all who resided there.

The King's palace was a spectacular sight. It stood tall on the highest point of the kingdom where everyone could see it. The peak of its steep roof towered some one hundred feet into the sky with smaller towers at each corner. The palace was so illuminated that you would think that a piece of the sun had fallen and rested upon the hilltop. The view from the palace was picturesque. On one side it overlooked the fields, the forest, and the sea. On the other, you could see the sparkling glow of a beautiful city that shone with the radiance and luster of the finest crystal. Inside the city were streets made of pure gold, yet transparent like glass. Surrounding the city was a great high wall with twelve gates. The walls were made of jasper with foundations decorated with many kinds of precious stones. Each of the twelve gates was made of a single pearl, carved and polished until it glistened with startling clarity. The vibrant river flowed out of the meadow and along the city street, then onward into the sea. Very unique houses lined the streets of gold, each designed according to its lodger's personal taste. Picture perfect, it was as if this city came to life out of a beautiful painting.

THE KINGDOM

The King cherished the grand city, but what He loved the most were those who lived in it. They were called *Malachs*, and they were His pride and joy. The King had created them to be His servants, but also His friends and companions. They talked and laughed with Him and loved to be in His presence. Now, the Malachs were created similar in nature to the King, though each of them had notably different personalities, gifts, talents, and strengths. They were created in various shapes and sizes; some were two feet tall with wings and little round bellies, while others were eight feet tall and built like strong oxen. Some could fly, and some only walked, but the ones who walked could also run and never tire. The Malachs were artists and musicians, builders and craftsmen. They helped the King sow and reap, gathering the harvest in due season. Many were master chefs, preparing the finest of meals. Others helped the King care for the animals. Some were messengers who carried the words of the King throughout the kingdom. And very few, only the elite, were guardians of the walls. These were the watchmen, the protectors. Only the King knew what lurked beyond the perimeter of the kingdom, and these chosen few stood ready to stand against this unknown force at any time.

Now, King Adonai was a great and mighty King made of pure light, exalted above all, and yet His nature was very loving and gentle. He was the creator of everything, all of His creation was good. The kingdom was perfect in every way—well, perfect, that is, to everyone except the King. Even though the King had beauty stretching from sky to sea, animals that gave Him joy, and loyal, hardworking Malachs who obeyed His every command, there was still one thing missing from the King's life that made this perfect kingdom imperfect to Him—the King had no family of His own. This was the King's one desire, and yet His one dilemma. He longed to have children made in His very image and likeness—not just another creation, but family birthed from the depth of His being that was truly a part of Him. Unfortunately, the King knew that creating beings of this stature could certainly come with great consequences. He knew that a creation of this magnitude, given a

REMEMBER

choice, could most emphatically start a rebellion and a struggle for power. For this reason, the King, from His infinite wisdom, made a way when there seemed to be no way. The impossible became possible. Alas, this is what started the rebellion.

THREE ARE CHOSEN

There was a definite bounce in the King's step that morning as He made His way to the city. He had decided to select three Malachs to help Him prepare for and teach His children after they were created. Yes, the King was creating a family! "Good morning, Jubil," announced the King as He stepped onto the golden street that followed the crystal stream.

Jubil lowered his large brown wings that had been creating his shade and raised his head off the cushion of grass to see if it was the King. "Good morning, my Lord," he replied. "I was just lying here composing a new song for you and enjoying this beautiful morning. Would you like to sit along the bank with me while I play my violin for you?"

"I would love to, Jubil; you are my greatest musician, and I would love to hear you play, but not this morning. Today I have something special I want to share with you. Come with me, and we'll go find Michael and Gabriel."

"Sure thing, my King," said Jubil joyfully. Jubil rose to his feet and stretched his masculine body, running his fingers through his perfect blonde hair. Precious stones and gems that covered his clothes reflected off the sun a multitude of colors. Jubil tucked his violin beneath his arm and slid his bow into its holster. The violin was more than an instrument to Jubil; it was a part of who he was. With one stroke of his bow, he could melt the heart of any listener.

Just up the road a ways, standing strong upon the great wall near the city gate, was Michael keeping watch. He was a mountain of a Malach, strongest and most powerful of them all. He didn't have wings as some did, but he could run with the speed of a lightning bolt.

"Are we safe today Michael?" said the King jokingly.

Michael raised his shield to block the bright rising sun and to see who was jeering him. His bold hairy cheeks jostled as he let out a bellowing laugh. "Yes, King Adonai," he replied in a low, rumbling voice. "Whenever you are here, we are always safe." Michael bound his shield to his broad back, let out a quick snort, and then leaped to the ground with a thunderous landing.

Jubil and the King admired his great strength. His cloven hooves, tightly woven dark hair, and the sturdy horns on his head made him appear like a bull, yet he stood erect like a Malach.

"How may I serve you this morning, King Adonai?" asked Michael.

"I need you to come with me this morning," said the King. "You are one of my elect, my chief protector and watcher of the walls. This morning I want you to come to my palace so I can share a surprise with you. Now come let's go find Gabriel."

"Did someone say my name?" asked a dark figure perched atop the bell tower. In a streak of light, Gabriel dove down toward them, and within inches he swerved upward, spread his long wings, and daintily stopped, precisely before the King.

"You sure know how to make a dramatic entrance!" said Michael.

"Yeah, watch the wind, Gabriel, you almost messed my hair up," said Jubil with a chuckle.

"That's why I've chosen you Gabriel. You, sir, are the master of the air, my chief messenger. I made you sleek and agile for that very reason, and you have definitely honed your skills."

"What is it that you desire of me this morning, your majesty?" asked Gabriel. The sunrays glistened off his long, coal black hair and his dark slender wings.

"I've been waiting for this day for a long time, planning and watching. I have chosen you three, because you have excelled above the rest. Jubil can play any instrument, and none can match his passion in worship. Michael has grown stronger than ten malachs, and you, Gabriel, fly like the wind. It is you three that will come live with me in my palace." The King turned and walked back toward His palace, smiling from ear to ear. He glowed brighter than the sun as He pranced away. The three Malachs stood with blank stares.

"Did you say live with you?" asked Jubil humbly.

"Yes!" shouted the King. "I said live with me; now, come on."

The three Malachs looked at each other, grinned, and then sped up to the King.

Along the way, the King briefly explained their new positions—not yet revealing to them that He was creating a family—telling them that they would live in His palace so they could develop their talents even greater.

Upon arrival, the King pushed the front doors open, and the Malachs were breathless. Before them was a dazzling foyer with marble floors, stone pillars, and large glass windows measuring fifty feet high, each trimmed with solid gold.

From the foyer, they entered the vast throne room in the center of the palace. The throne room was even more majestic than the foyer. It was a huge room, circular in shape, with white granite walls and evenly spaced golden pillars stretching upward, and then angling in to form the peak of the roof. The height of the ceiling was so tall that it was hard to see where the golden supports met at the highest point. Encircling the throne room were black granite stairs that ascended to a heavenly loft with golden rails and spindles that twisted and turned. Prisms of light danced through the etched, stained glass windows high above the rails and two glass doors, one on each side of the loft, opened to a balcony with an eagle's eye view of the entire kingdom. The floor of the throne room looked like a sea of dark glass. Smoke rose from it, swirling around their feet as they walked. At a particular corner in the room they noticed that the floor seemed to be moving. "There it is," said the King. "That is where the crystal river begins, and its life giving-power originates."

REMEMBER

Michael knelt beside the churning spring, cupped his hands, scooped up some water and drank. The living water bubbled inside his belly causing him to giggle.

Jubil and Gabriel looked unsure whether the King wanted them to drink. The King nodded and said, "This is your home boys, drink all you desire!"

In the heart of the room was an enormous throne constructed of pure gold with a rainbow encircling it. Six steps led up to the throne, and each step had a golden lion at the end, twelve in all. On each side of the throne were two winged creatures, each with one wing stretched forward to form the armrest, and the other wing stretched overhead, touching in the center, forming a canopy above the throne. As they approached the throne, the Malachs noticed that it began to glow and became brighter the closer the King got to it, as if it was alive, sensing His presence. They marveled at the sight of it and felt a tingling sensation in their bodies that was unfamiliar.

Their attention was then drawn to a wonderful blue light flooding through a golden, framed doorway.

"Look at that," said Jubil, walking toward it. Every jewel on his clothes sparkled as he entered through the door.

Jubil was dwarfed by its size; the corridor was as wide as a city street, and the ceiling was clear as glass, revealing the gorgeous blue sky above, which created the glow seen from the throne room. Lining the corridor were many doors, with three of them displaying an engraving of each of their names, Michael, Gabriel, and Jubil. Curious, each of them went and stood in front of their own door, and, simultaneously, turned the golden doorknobs. The King grinned and watched the look on their faces as the doors opened to an entire mansion, fully furnished and decorated to each of their individual tastes.

The Malachs gazed inside their wonderful new homes, hesitating for a moment before entering. Immediately, they took a double take down the long hallway and noticed that each door had names embossed on them as well—names they did not recognize. The

Malachs looked at each other, shrugged their shoulders, and then entered through their own door.

Jubil walked in and smiled. The shape and texture of the ceiling and walls were a perfect acoustical design. Jubil pulled out his violin and began to play. Colors accompanied the music and displayed an elegant mix of the softest sound with a pleasant light show. "Exquisite," said Jubil.

Michael slammed into his room, and the walls were soft and cushiony, silencing his aggressive entrance. With the touch of a button, the floor became a treadmill with endless speeds. The lamps were made of barbells, and the couch was fastened to pulleys so Michael could lift himself while he relaxed. "Awesome!" said Michael

Gabriel admired his bright blue walls and chairs in the shapes of billowy clouds. The ceilings were very high, and trampolines lined each wall. "Sweet!" he said .

After they explored their new homes and settled in, the King called for them to appear before Him in His throne room. When they arrived, the King was seated on His throne, and oh, what a sight He was to see. Rainbow colored light shot out in all directions. The King's body was like bronze glowing in a furnace, and His face was like the sun shining in all its brilliance. In awkward suspense, each came and stood before Him as His great power riveted through their bodies. They trembled before Him and became so weak, they could barely remain upright.

The King pulled out a small vial with special oil in it. He slowly poured a portion of it on each of their heads and laid His hands on them. Although they didn't know what He was doing, He was anointing them, allowing His creative powers to supernaturally give them the ability to fulfill the extraordinary positions that He had chosen for them. As He did so, His power fell on them with so much force that they immediately found themselves on the floor, face down before Him. They could barely lift their heads to look at Him, trying desperately anyway. They strained to see Him, squinting while covering their eyes with their hands. His light was much too bright.

What a privilege to be here! thought the Malachs.

As they lay there, the King spoke to each of them with a voice of many rushing waters and said, "I have chosen you three and anointed you to receive a portion of my power, wisdom, and knowledge. Gabriel, I am anointing you to be my head messenger, prince of the air. You will teach your Malachs to fly with great speed, for you are wise and swift in flight. You will be a messenger, not only in this kingdom, but to a people of another land. To you, I give a portion of my secret knowledge to assist you in the duties I have established for you." The King then presented Gabriel with a special trumpet and said, "You will use this instrument when you need to gather the Malachs, and to someday gather my new creation as well."

The King went over to Michael next and said, "Michael, I am anointing you to be my chief protector, guardian prince. You will instruct your Malachs to watch over my new creation. You will teach these Malachs the art of fighting, to be master horsemen, and to run like the wind. They must become mighty in battle as you are mighty, brave as you are brave, and strong as you are strong. Teach them to wield the sword and draw the bow. For in time, they will be used to protect my new creation and impart this wisdom to them as well. To you, I give a portion of my secret wisdom. With this you will lead vast armies in the unavoidable war."

"War?" Michael asked. "What is war?"

The King hesitated momentarily, allowing the anointing oil to take effect so that Michael could understand. Almost instantly, the oil released the secret wisdom, and in detail different aspects of warfare were revealed to Michael, from one on one combat to great strategic maneuvers with vast armies. Through the vision, Michael saw bows, arrows, swords, spears, and other instruments of battle. He, instantly, not only knew how to use them, but how to make them as well. He was very enthusiastic about these new feats of strength. It seemed like a new and exciting game to him, one that he was quite sure he could do very well.

Finally, the King turned to Jubil and said, "Jubil, I have chosen you to be my lead worshiper, prince of praise. Never has any Malach worshipped me with the same passion as you. You will play music for all who enter my throne room, teaching them to worship. When they do, my anointing will be released to strengthen them. You will teach your Malachs to do the same. To you, I give a portion of my secret power which you will impart unto my new creation."

When the King finished speaking, the light around Him diminished. The three of them lay there motionless, until His anointing subsided. Slowly, they each stood up. When they looked at each other, they saw a subtle glow. Though not nearly as bright as their King, still a faint light came forth from each Malach.

They turned to the King, and with wonder in their eyes and excitement in their voices, asked in unison, "Who is this new creation? And what will its purpose be?"

The King enthusiastically began to share the plans of His new family with them. "I have lived many years in this kingdom, more than you could know. And though I have many friends surrounding me, I have always lived in this palace alone. Now the time has come for me to create children, beings like me, created in my image, with no other purpose than to be my family. So I have made arrangements to do so, and you three will play a part. Take the gifts that I have given you and start perfecting them. Choose those that will assist you, for soon my children will need your help to grow to maturity."

"Yes, your Majesty," said Michael optimistically. "This is incredible. I can't wait to meet your new family!"

Without any questions, Michael and Gabriel hurriedly left to start preparing for their missions.

Not Jubil; he stood fast, desiring to ask the King one more question. Most innocently, with a tender look, and concern in his voice, he asked, "Why, Lord? Why don't you make us your family? Why don't you make us to be like you?"

Lovingly, the King reached out and put His hands on Jubil's shoulders. "Jubil, you are beautifully and wonderfully made, the apple of my eye. Please don't think that my new family will diminish my love for you. I know that you have questions and concerns, Jubil; however, you must trust that I know what I am doing. You have always been a loyal servant and a friend to me. Now go and serve me as you have in the past."

"Yes, Lord," Jubil replied. "I shall trust and serve you well. I shall master the power of worship, and I will teach it to your children when they arrive."

Jubil turned and walked away while the King hung His head, mindful of the inevitable.

THE BLEMISH

Michael, Gabriel, and Jubil were like little boys in a candy shop. They were so thrilled about their new assignments that they could hardly contain their emotions. They met in the foyer to begin their journey into the city to choose their apprentices.

Gabriel looked at Michael and Jubil and said with a grin, "Sorry, I can't wait on you slow pokes; I've got to fly."

Gabriel leaped into the air and began to push off with his long wings, but before he could get very far, Michael jumped up, and like a frog snatching food with its tongue, grabbed his foot and flung him to the ground. Gabriel rolled backwards on the floor as Michael made a dash for the door.

Michael yelled back, "Looks like you two will be eating my dust!"

Right then, Michael looked up and saw Jubil darting through a window, spreading his large wings to take flight.

"Sorry, Michael," Jubil crowed, "I don't have much of an appetite for dust!" The King laughed hysterically as He watched the three of them make their exits.

As they entered the city, the other Malachs gathered to admire their new appearance.

"Look, they're glowing," one said.

"They glow like the King," said another.

First Jubil, then Michael and Gabriel started speaking one by one, telling them how the King had chosen them for a special assignment.

"The King brought us into His chambers. He has shown us great things!" said Michael. "He is planning to create a family and has chosen us to help Him teach them."

Then Jubil emphasized. "The best news is that each of you will get to help too."

"Wow!" said one of the Malachs. "The King is creating a new family. Will they look like us?"

"Actually," said Gabriel, "The King said they would be made in His image, just like Him. I would imagine they will be the spitting image of the King."

Immediately, everyone squeezed in line and raised their hands, hoping they would be picked to help. Soon after the three selected their Malachs, training commenced.

Gabriel began teaching his messengers how to fly like the wind, straight up into the sky and then back down. He showed them how to dart to the left and then to the right, zigzagging through the sky. They trained by racing the birds, and soon the fastest falcon could not dive with equal speed, pigeons couldn't dodge as quickly, nor the greatest eagle soar with the same stamina. They became the champions of the sky. For fun they would dive into the clouds that looked like fluffy pillows, and as they would pierce through the bottom of them, they would leave a hole in the center making them look like giant frosted donuts. Other times they would fly by a cloud so fast that the cloud would be sucked in by the draft and with artistic twists and turns they would shape it into words that glorified the King. As the King watched from the window in the highest point of His palace, He felt greatly honored.

Gabriel's job was fairly easy. Michael, on the other hand, had a much bigger task ahead of him. He gathered the Malachs he had chosen, starting with the watchmen, and told them that he was going to teach them about warfare.

"Warfare?" many questioned. "What is warfare?"

Michael laughed since he had reacted the same way. Then he assured them that they would understand once he explained everything. He started off by teaching them about the weapons they would use and how they would make them. The Malachs went right to work crafting powerful, yet elegant swords, the finest of which was crafted for the King Himself. Each sword was so strong that it could split stones like they were bread, yet it would never dull the edge of the blade. Michael then taught them how to make bows and arrows. Each bow was crafted from a special type of wood that was very light and flexible, while remaining strong as iron. The wood was carved very decoratively and lined with pure gold. One silver strand was formed to make the drawstring. Thousands upon thousands of arrows were made with the greatest precision, the sharpest tips, and the most colorful feathers. Lastly, they made spectacular shields and armor crafted of silver, and polished till they gleamed.

Once all the weapons and armor were finished, it was time for Michael to begin training his warriors. He started by showing them how to run with great speed and agility. They would practice by racing the horses through the hillside, the deer through the woods, and the cheetahs through the tall grass. Like the messengers in the air, no animal could compare with them in speed or agility. They could run like lightning, stop on a dime, and turn ninety degrees without slowing down. They could run so fast that they were able to run up the side of a tree, turn, and come back down without ever falling.

Next, Michael started teaching them hand-to-hand combat, swordsmanship and archery. As he spoke, his words imparted to them the secret wisdom concerning warfare that the King had given him. Michael paired them up and taught them how to use a sword, and, in time, each of them became a master swordsman.

The Malachs then moved on to practicing with the bows and arrows, learning very quickly. The first one to shoot was amazed! The bow was very easy to draw back, but when released, the arrow traveled at lightning speed, striking the target with a dead bull's-eye.

"Wow, that was a great shot," said Michael. "Do you think you can do that again? Better yet, how about when the target's moving?" The two laughed.

Suddenly, Michael's laughter faded. The magnitude of warfare was becoming a reality. This was more than just a game; Malachs were going to be hurt, which even with the King's secret wisdom, was hard for him to fully perceive. Michael, nor any of the Malachs, had ever known pain or sorrow.

"We must train harder!" shouted Michael. "We will practice again and again until no target is a challenge for us!"

As training continued, each of them gained great skill, strength, and endurance, learning how to maneuver as an army of one. Michael taught them that when they operated in unity they had a greater advantage than in fighting alone.

In the courtyard, Jubil was busy training the Malachs that he had chosen to become musicians and worshippers. He was teaching them how to make every kind of instrument that the King had inspired in him. The King had given them gold, silver, and the finest wood to use for their creations. The Malachs caught on quickly, and as the days proceeded, they made hundreds of instruments.

Jubil then imparted his secret power into them, and they began to play music with great intensity, bringing the King's anointing into their presence. With each advancing day, their talents progressed, and joy filled their hearts as the time drew closer for the King to create His children. Jubil, on the other hand, found himself struggling to stay focused on what he was doing. Wry thoughts were continually popping in his head concerning the King's children.

Why, thought Jubil. *Why am I thinking this way—again? This morning I was brimming over with joy, and now I feel apathy creeping in. Why am I being tormented so?*

Jubil, while wrestling with his thoughts, instructed the Malachs to continue practicing until the end of the day, then he slipped away, back to his room. The Malachs were so excited about playing their instruments and being immersed in the King's presence that

THE BLEMISH

they hardly noticed Jubil's departure. While at home, Jubil sat on his bed, mulling things over, trying to sort out his feelings.

"The King is creating a new family," said Jubil under his breath. "I know I should be excited, so why don't I feel joy like the others? They light up at the mere mention of the children, yet I struggle with the whole idea of it."

Jubil had never felt this way before. Until now, he had always understood that he was somehow special, possibly the King's favorite. Jubil had always assumed that the King loved him just a little more than the rest of the Malachs. Now he felt that this was no longer going to be the case. These new children would be better than him, stronger than him, and more like the King than he ever would be. Surely, the King would love them more!

"What am I going to do?" he murmured.

Pondering these thoughts, Jubil's stomach twisted in knots, and then his side began to itch. Without thinking, he scratched his side, and when he did, he felt something odd. Looking down, he noticed a rough, gray, dry patch on his skin. The light which was emanating from his body had grown dull in that area. Jubil cringed at the sight of the dark, ugly spot. He jumped up in great distress and got a closer look in the mirror. He had never seen spots like that on anyone in the entire kingdom. The kingdom was perfect, and he had always been perfect, without any blemishes. As he stared into the mirror, a look of confusion covered his face.

Where did this spot come from? thought Jubil. *What does this mean?* He quickly covered the blemish, pulling his vest down over it again, wanting to forget that it ever existed, and hoping it would be gone when morning dawned.

The next morning, he anxiously reached down and felt for the blemish, hoping that it had only been a dream. Doing so, he realized that the grotesque spot was still there. Now panic was setting in.

Jubil cried out, "I can't let anyone see me this way. What will they think?" He paced back and forth frantically, continuously opening his robe, looking at the blemish, and then quickly covering it up again.

"No one must know about this, not even the King!" said Jubil. He quickly prepared for the oncoming day. Not wanting to look upon his disgusting malformation anymore, he left his room and made his way to the throne room. The King was already seated on His throne when Jubil arrived. Jubil, very nervously, picked up his violin and began to play before any of the other Malachs got there.

As soon as he did, the King stopped him and asked, "Have you been thinking about my children, Jubil?"

Jubil paused for a moment; his face revealed that he was startled by the King's question. Knots tightened in the pit of his belly. With uneasiness in his voice, he answered the King, "Yes Lord, I too am anticipating your family's arrival, just like everyone else."

"That is good, Jubil," the King replied. "So tell me this, in your anticipation, do you feel the goodness of joy, or do you feel the unpleasantness of fear of the unknown?"

"Lord, what do you mean, I don't understand?" said Jubil, turning his blemished side away from the King.

Then the King stood up and told Jubil to come closer. He put His arms around him, and said, "Jubil, I know you don't know the word fear, but have you perhaps experienced its unpleasantness on the inside of you?"

Jubil lowered his head. The King grasped Jubil's face with His hands and looked deep into his eyes. "I want you to know, Jubil, that you can stop the pain you feel if you will stop certain thoughts you have been entertaining. Listen to me very carefully! If you will turn your thoughts over to me, I will take them away, and you will feel relief. Then the blemish on your side will be gone. If you should decide to hold on to these ugly thoughts and continue to listen to them, they will begin to change you from within. Each thought will give birth to evil, which in turn, will produce darkness."

"Evil?" asked Jubil, looking distraught.

"Yes, evil," responded the King. "This evil that you have been feeling inside is called jealousy. It is caused by feeling misfortune

THE BLEMISH

by another's good fortune. It is what is making you feel sick. Left alone, eventually it will devour your soul and destroy you."

Jubil, frightened by the King's words, shook frantically, "No, Lord, this cannot be! I do not want this darkness inside of me. I want to keep the light you have given me. Please, Lord, I do not want to be destroyed. I only thought you would love your children more than you love me. I have always felt like I was special and that you loved me more than the rest. Now your children will be greater than me." Jubil's heart was stirred, and he wept before the King.

The King pulled Jubil close to His chest and said, "Jubil, you know I love you dearly. You are my pride and joy, just like all of my Malachs. I am no respecter of persons. Please believe me, when my children come to live with me, I will not love you any less, nor will I love them any more. My love is not based on one's performance or ability. I love each of you because I created you, and you are mine. Nothing you do will change the amount of love I have for you. You only need to be yourself; be who I created you to be."

As he was being held, Jubil felt a wet sensation sliding down his cheek. "What is this?" he asked.

The King smiled and gently said, "It's called a tear, Jubil."

The King wiped away Jubil's tear and immediately his side was healed.

"What is a tear?" asked Jubil, still curious about this strange liquid.

"A tear is an expression of emotion that has been stirred within you. It is produced by feelings of sadness and sorrow or love and joy, and right now I believe you're experiencing both sadness and joy."

Suddenly, the tan color of Jubil's skin returned, replacing the gray blemish. The familiar smile appeared back on Jubil's face, and he looked like his old self again, ready to worship his wonderful, merciful King. As he started to play, glorious bliss filled the room, and smoke began rising from the floor. Jubil fell at the King's feet, worshipping Him and thanking Him for all that He had done.

IN HIS IMAGE

There was a hush over the kingdom that morning while everyone eagerly awaited the event that was about to take place. The hard work preparing for the King's children was at last finished.

As the King entered the throne room, He called to His servants, "Jubil, Michael, Gabriel—it is time to—"

But before He could finish the sentence, all three were already making a mad dash down the corridor toward Him. When they arrived before the King's throne, He made His announcement.

"Today is the day that I will create my children. Go and share the good news with my kingdom. Blow your trumpet, Gabriel, and gather all the Malachs in the courtyard."

"With pleasure, Lord. This is what we have been waiting for," said Gabriel.

He gave his trumpet a blast, and the sound of thunder echoed throughout the kingdom. The Malachs knew what this sound was; for they had been impatiently, but eagerly, anticipating this moment as well. Within minutes, every Malach had made their way to the courtyard and gathered as close as possible to see this wonderful event. They were overwhelmed with joy.

Gabriel instructed his messengers to fly above the courtyard so they could see the new arrivals. Michael gathered his warriors in formation in the center of the courtyard, and Jubil gathered with his musicians on each side of the platform where the King stood. The King was grateful to see everyone's enthusiasm. He stepped forward and started the ceremony.

Jubil and his musicians began to play with great vigor. Sounds of celebration filled the air as the King stood in preparation to create. As the Malachs watched in awe, the King spoke the first name.

"Aaron," He said in a loud, commanding voice. When He did, a portion of light came out of the King's bosom and appeared before them.

"Oooohh," said the crowd.

As each eye fixated on the light, it suddenly began to change to a smoky mist.

"Aaaahhhh," said the Malachs, quite intrigued.

The dark mist hovered in the air for just a moment, and then it began to transform into a loose clay like figure. Everyone watched with widened eyes and mouths agape. The figure continued to solidify into what appeared to be the King's first child.

"Welcome, Aaron," said the King. He was very proud.

Aaron stood with a puzzled look on his face. Curling his hand into a fist, he rubbed his eyes and then looked at all the Malachs staring back at him. Everyone's attention was on Aaron. He was a dark, handsome man with black curly hair, dressed in nothing more than a simple white robe. Everyone stared at Aaron with excitement, and then suddenly their excitement was replaced by a look of disappointment. Aaron was beautiful and wonderfully made, but he was not what they expected. He was not nearly as big as the King. He didn't look powerful, and he didn't glow with a brilliant light. It was obvious that he was the King's offspring, but he paled in comparison. In fact, he even looked weaker than some of the Malachs. He was smaller than many of them, he didn't have wings to fly, and he didn't look like he could run with great speed.

The Malachs stood gawking at Aaron as if dumbfounded by his appearance. The King, on the other hand, was well pleased and continued speaking names, and thusly created more children quite similar to Aaron.

"Eden, Gary, Karen, Adelynn, Faith, Austin, Sydni, Sophia, Mia, Amber, Alyssa, Kaelin, Malachi, Eleya, Lyric, Josiah, Azariah, Isaac, Kara, David, Alex, Ava, Avery, Ciarah, Kieley, Elijah, Korik, and Adam." On and on He continued speaking until He had finished creating all of His children. He saw all that He had made, and it was very good!

Thousands of the King's children stood before them, each one unique and different. There were tall and short, big and small children with different colored skin and hair. What stood out the most, though, was that half of the children seemed to be bigger and stronger, while the other half seemed to be smaller and frail. The Malachs looked them over very closely, and then looked to the King, as if needing an explanation.

Knowing their thoughts, the King spoke up. "Standing before you are my children." The King's eyes sparkled with excitement. "They are more than just a creation. They are my offspring made in my very image, each made from a portion of myself. Because of this, I will call them *Zera*, for they are my seed, my royal family. They are a chosen generation, and more than conquerors! I know they look very weak to you right now, but in time, when they reach maturity, they will truly be just like me. Until then, there is much that they must learn, experience, and endure. Do not let what you see fool you, for they are more powerful than they appear. Notice the ones that seem stronger; these are the males. The others that seem frailer are the females. Alone they can do many things, but when they come together as one, they can become enough like me to create a new life."

The Malachs looked at the King's new sons and daughters with even greater amazement and respect. *Wow*, they thought, *the Zera can create new life just like the King.*

The Zera, on the other hand, still apparently puzzled, looked down at their bodies, noticing their feet and toes, holding out their hands, wiggling their fingers. They looked at each other and noticed they each had different faces and different bodies. Then they looked at all the Malachs and at the glorious King standing before them. A look of joy glowed from their smiling faces, causing celebration to break out once again throughout the courtyard. Spontaneous dancing, shouting, and singing erupted among the Malachs and Zera alike. The King clapped and cheered for His creation.

The messengers, along with Gabriel, began to fly in synchronization over and under each other, making dynamic dives, twists, and stunts in the air in celebration. Michael and the warriors began running, leaping, and doing acrobatic flips. It was all so magnificent to watch. The performance was excellently orchestrated with great precision. Suddenly, Jubil began to play music, and all the musicians accompanied him. The music was so exuberating that all of the King's creation began to praise Him. The Malach's danced before Him, the grass and the trees swayed back and forth, the river bubbled in tune, and the animals joined in with joyful songs. Suddenly, the Zera fell to the ground, consumed by the King's power, and began to laugh uncontrollably. Oh, how His presence made them feel. They seemed to thrive from it as if it was life to their bodies and food to their souls. All of them at once began to express with words of adoration and praise their love to their father, creator, and King.

When the day ended, the King dismissed the Malachs and escorted the Zera, along with Michael, Jubil, and Gabriel, into the palace where He had prepared their homes. As the Zera entered, they looked amazed by the beauty that surrounded them. It was all so very new to them, and yet they had a feeling as if they had been there before, as if it had always been their home. After touring the palace, the King took them into the corridor.

"Look, it has my name on it," said Gary with surprise. Before him stood a magnificent door with his name engraved on a gold plaque.

Each of them saw Gary's name on the door, then excitedly searched for their own and began reading their names out loud. Michael, Gabriel, Jubil, along with the King, were greatly amused. The excitement was contagious.

"Go inside," said the King. "It was created just for you."

THE FALL

Early the next morning, at the King's request, Gabriel gave his horn a loud blast, and then waited for the Zera to come racing out of their rooms. After a few moments, no one appeared. He blew the trumpet again, and still no one responded.

"What's going on? Where is everyone?" questioned Gabriel, lifting his dark eyebrows. Curiosity getting the best of him, he went to each door and knocked; still, no one answered. He listened at each door, not able to hear anyone stirring. Gabriel was getting frustrated, so he opened their doors one at a time.

Where are they? he thought. *How strange. I know I watched everyone go home last night. Where could they be?*

Gabriel ran faster than he ever had before to the throne room, shouting, "King Adonai, King Adonai!"

When he entered the room, to his surprise, all of the Zera were already seated around the throne talking with the King. Gabriel was a bit embarrassed.

Michael looked at him and said, "Where have you been, sleepy head?" He tried hard not to laugh, but a few snorts and chuckles slipped out anyway.

"I was looking for the Zera," said Gabriel defensively.

Everyone held their tongue, as Michael and Jubil snickered. Soon Gabriel, being a good sport, let down his guard and all of them had a good laugh.

The King then said, "Thanks for the announcement this morning. Unfortunately, none of the Zera could sleep last night. They were much too excited about their first day in the kingdom. Now that you are here, you, along with Michael and Jubil, can take them on their grand tour."

Michael and Jubil threw an arm around Gabriel to show their friendly truce, and then motioned for the Zera to join them. They took them first to the crystal river where they waded in the soft flowing current and splashed each other with the cool refreshing water. The Zera loved the water and knew it was special as soon as they stepped into it. It felt so vibrant that it seemed alive. Instead of flowing around them, it felt as if it was flowing right through them. Some of the Zera tried drinking the water, and when they did, it tasted as sweet as honey and tingled in their bellies. They learned much about the kingdom while they played and had fun. They met all the animals in the fields and the forest. They spoke with them for a while, and then they ran and played, stopping at each new attraction. They ran the green grass between their toes and the tall golden grasses through their fingers. They climbed the trees and hung upside down by their knees. They climbed so far out to the ends of the branches that the long thin supple limbs gently lowered them down to the ground. After running through the forest, they made their way out to the sea where they fed the fish and sea creatures.

As they made their way back to the palace, they skipped along laughing and singing, frolicking through the meadows, taking in all the beautiful sights. The birds, butterflies, and the flowers all displayed their brilliant colors. As they walked along, they noticed the flowers and grass that were stepped on seemed to bounce back to their original position.

Jubil, however, saw something else that caught his attention. Under closer observation, he noticed as the Zera were walking along, the grass leaned toward them, just as it did the King, ever so slightly, though, as if the grass somehow saw the King in them. At first, it was kind of nice to Jubil. He started to share it with the other Malachs, but before he could open his mouth, a thought popped into his head. Quite innocently he wondered, *Why doesn't the grass lean toward me?* It was then that pride began to creep into his heart, like a shadow replacing the light of a setting sun.

"I have great power," said Jubil under his breath. "In fact, I am better than they are; I have wings, I am strong and more beautiful, so why doesn't the grass lean toward me when I walk by?"

Jubil had forgotten about the thoughts he had entertained in his room prior to being healed by the King, and now they were flooding his mind. Jubil should have heeded the King's warning, instead, he felt like the King was purposely trying to keep something from him.

Why doesn't the King want me to think these thoughts? pondered Jubil. *He told me that these thoughts would destroy me, yet I'm still alive. In fact, I feel more alive now. I don't feel confused any more, for the first time I feel as if I finally see clearly.*

In seconds, the darkness grasped hold of Jubil's mind, and what had started out innocently, now exploded into something very evil.

I get it now, thought Jubil, his eyes lighting up. *The King wants me to teach the Zera so they can be greater than me.*

"THIS CAN NEVER HAPPEN!" screamed Jubil at the top of his lungs.

Everyone stopped and looked at him.

"What can never happen?" asked Michael inquisitively.

"Oh," said Jubil, nearly blushing at his outburst. "I guess I was thinking out loud." Jubil tried to get everyone laughing, hoping they would forget what they had heard.

All the way home he pretended to be happy, singing and skipping along with the others. However, once Jubil was in the privacy of his mansion, he opened up his heart to every hateful thought that came to him. Like a mighty rushing river, these thoughts flooded his soul.

I have always been the greatest Malach in the kingdom, thought Jubil. *Why should I train the Zera to take my place? I can't teach them what I know. In fact, I need to know everything that Michael and Gabriel are teaching them. When I have gained all of that knowledge and wisdom, I will be the greatest in the kingdom again. Then the King will notice me and see that I am His finest creation.*

Every kind of jealousy, greed, pride, and anger poured into Jubil's heart. Spots and blemishes began forming on different parts of his body. Jubil noticed the changes taking place, but it didn't seem to bother him at all. He was now embracing each new thought, each one more corrupt than the next. At once, a thought came to him that was the wickedest of them all. In desperation, he tried to dismiss it, but again and again the thought showed its ugly head. Jubil tried to resist. It was futile. The temptation overtook him, and, with a sinister smile and a strange look in his eye, he thought, *Not only will I be greater than the Zera, I will be greater than the King Himself.*

Jubil collected his thoughts. "No!" he shouted, gripping his head with his hands, shaking with confusion, feeling very distraught. *I must not think anything like that. I love the King. I would never want to take His place.*

Now pacing back and forth in his room, Jubil began arguing with himself.

There is no way I would ever want anything like that to happen. I just want the King to love me the most. I need His love the most.

Then Jubil, as if his mind was becoming infected by a poison spreading rapidly through his veins said, "I have always served the King loyally, and what have I gotten in return?"

Just as suddenly, a tiny bit of light once again revealed itself in Jubil, reminding him of that morning he spent with the King in the throne room.

The King told me that He would not love me any less. He has given me great power and a mansion in His palace. Shouldn't I be thankful for that?

Again the darkness took control.

Yes, but now He is going to give it all to the Zera, and once He uses us to teach them, He will do away with us.

The evil desire increased in power, and soon every bit of light that Jubil had ever known was finally choked out.

Jubil's head began to explode with newly corrupted thoughts and emotions.

That's right! That's probably been the King's plan all along! He doesn't love us! He only wants to use us! I can't let this happen! I have to stop Him! I have to stop Him now! He's not going to pull a fast one on me. I will fight for what is rightfully mine. I will become the greatest in this kingdom and all will worship me! Yes, I will be greater than the King Himself! Jubil's eyes were bulging, veins popped out of his forehead, and a haunting laughter filled the room. It was creepy, bellowing out from the depths of his darkened soul. Jubil knew he was changing. He felt as if he was becoming more powerful with each and every new thought; still, he sensed that there was one more step that had to be taken. He quickly realized that the seed sown in his heart would have to be birthed through his mouth. It was obvious now that in order to complete the transformation, he would have to speak out loud what he was thinking in his heart. Jubil was learning the secret power of creating with his words. The power was in his tongue.

At once, he looked down at all the blemishes that were appearing on his body, and all he could do was laugh. He didn't care anymore. He looked up toward the ceiling, arms outstretched, palms facing upward, and with all the strength he could draw from his wicked heart, as if he was breaking chains that bound his soul and freeing himself from what he saw as a prison, he shouted at the top of his lungs, "I will be the greatest in this Kingdom!"

Sounds of cracking and popping filled the room as Jubil's body immediately began a transformation into a hideous creature covered with scales. His eyes became blood red with dark slits like that of a viper. His skin turned pasty gray in color and was rough to the touch. His fingers developed into claws, and his voice sounded deep and hollow. His teeth formed into long, pointy fangs, and all of his hair fell out. His wings became leathery, and spikes began forming down his back like that of a great dragon.

At the very instant he shouted those words, the King wept, and the kingdom shook violently, causing everyone to awaken from

THE FALL

their sleep. They looked around quite startled, wondering what had just occurred, but soon they each drifted back off to sleep. After a while, the only ones who were still awake were Jubil, who was in his room admiring his new look, and the King, sitting quietly on His throne. The King was dismal as He sat staring at the floor. It was a heart-wrenching moment for Him! There had never been anything like this in His kingdom. It had always been perfect, but was no longer so. What the King had so closely guarded the kingdom against, now found a door to enter through the heart of Jubil. The King wasn't surprised. He knew it was going to happen; nevertheless, seeing it destroy His precious Jubil hurt Him deeply. As another tear dripped from His eye and fell to the ground, the floor shook violently once again. This time the King waved his hand, prohibiting the sound and vibration from disturbing the rest of the kingdom.

In the meantime, back in his room, Jubil began making plans to overthrow the King. He knew he would have to be inconspicuous at first and hide his new identity from all the others. He surely did not want anyone to be able to see his hideous form and find out about his betrayal. If the other Malachs saw him this way, they wouldn't trust him, and he needed them to trust him more now than ever. Jubil knew he would have to change back into his original appearance, so he spoke, and his body began to alter again. Rattle—Crack—Pop.

"My disguise must be so convincing that even the King Himself cannot tell the difference," said Jubil.

He practiced changing form throughout the night, while making fake gestures and smiles in the mirror, so he would always seem to appear cheerful and polite, even though in his heart he was filled with bitterness and hatred for the King and the Zera.

SEEDS ARE SOWN

A dense mist swirled around Jubil as the morning dawned. His eyes pierced the darkness with tiny lightning bolts flashing out of them. Fire danced about his tongue, and smoke drifted out of his teeth like fog weaving through reeds in a sparse, dank swamp. Realizing it was morning, Jubil regained his composure one last time, transforming back into the Jubil everyone knew and loved. As he glanced back at the mirror, his nose cringed in disgust; he put on a happy face, and then made his way to the throne room. All the Zera, along with the Malachs, were gathered there waiting for him to start the worship. Smiling from ear to ear, he picked up his instrument of choice, the violin, and began to play as if nothing had transpired. With each stroke of his bow, the music altered the atmosphere, captivating the very soul of those who listened. As if enraptured, they each fell before the King in worship.

As Jubil played, he closed his eyes and imagined that everyone was giving him praise instead of King Adonai. As he took it all in, an evil grin revealed how much he loved this feeling of complete power. The lure of it seemed to envelope him as he coveted the King's position. Jubil became lost in the moment as he played with great passion and intensity, but when he opened his eyes and saw all the Zera and Malachs worshipping the King instead of him, anger and jealousy began to well up in his spiteful soul. Jubil was filled with rage, yet somehow he managed to keep his emotions at bay.

"Soon all of this will be mine," said Jubil, mumbling under his breath. Then, begrudgingly, Jubil fell down before the King and pretended to worship Him as well. As he did, he was the only one

SEEDS ARE SOWN

who knew what he was really thinking, or so he thought. As the music and praise ended, everyone hurried along to continue where they had left off the day before. Jubil, now controlled by his pride and arrogance, lagged just a little behind, not quite so eager.

Just before Jubil exited the door into the courtyard, the King called to him, "Jubil, please don't rush off just yet. Come and let me look at you."

Jubil stopped in his tracks; his heart began to beat faster and faster, feeling as if it was coming out of his chest.

Before he could turn around, the King said, "You played very well this morning Jubil; wouldn't you agree?"

Jubil lightened up a little. "Why, yes, your majesty," he replied, slowly turning around to look at the King, displaying a fake smile.

"In fact, you played exceptionally well this morning," said the King. "Come here; let me see you up close."

Jubil walked over to the King, trying to stay calm while retaining his facade, hoping He wouldn't notice anything different about him, he kept a safe distance between them. The King stepped closer, putting His illuminated hand on Jubil's shoulder. Butterflies rose in Jubil's stomach as the King began to speak.

"How is everything going, Jubil? How are things progressing with the Zera?"

Jubil quickly responded, trying to say the right things, "Everything is going very well, Lord, just as planned. I am excited for you and the Zera, you know that." At that, he hugged the King and kissed Him on His cheek.

"Yes, Jubil, I know you are," said the King, making eye contact with him.

Jubil, feeling very uneasy, tried desperately to retain his beautiful form. With all of his strength, he fought the temptation of transforming into the hideous beast that he really was. Turning away from the King, his eyes flickered to that of a viper and back again.

The King pretended not to notice while responding, "I'm glad to hear that everything is going so well!"

Walking away, Jubil said ever so sweetly, "Yes, Lord, everything is turning out better than I expected."

Jubil joined Michael and Gabriel in the courtyard. He listened and observed how their eyes sparkled while they spoke of the King. He then noticed that the Zera displayed the same emotion. The sight of it sickened Jubil, and the only way he could stomach it was to imagine that they were talking about him instead of the King, his head filling with vain ideas once again.

Michael, Gabriel, and Jubil, accompanied by their Malachs, each took a group of Zera and began teaching them. Jubil definitely did not have his heart in his work, but nevertheless, started with lessons in worship, imparting the King's power to the Zera. He then quickly chose another Malach, Basil, to take his place. He told Basil that he had other important matters to attend to, assuring him that he was the best for the job, making him feel quite important.

You see, Jubil really wanted to sneak off and absorb what Michael and Gabriel were teaching. So he continued to make up excuses day after day, leaving Basil in charge. He would then hide behind trees and rocks, slithering like a snake, just so he could eavesdrop on everything Michael and Gabriel were teaching the Zera, thereby attaining the secret wisdom and knowledge for himself.

Each evening, when they had finished training the Zera, Jubil would sneak down into the city to where he had once lived, and begin spreading evil seeds of thought among some of his closest friends. He didn't tell them about his transformation or his plans to take over the kingdom just yet, for his mission was to plant a thought in each of their minds to cause doubt and suspicion toward the King.

Jubil, outwardly innocent, said things like, "Do you think the King will love the Zera more than He loves us?" Then he would leave and allow time for his evil seed to take root. Each time he saw them, he watered his seeds by speaking more negative words over them.

He would say, "What if the King planned to replace us with these new creatures all along?"

Soon Jubil's wicked suggestions germinated and began to spread like a virus in the minds and souls of many Malachs. Once they believed what he was saying, they too began transforming just as Jubil had—first on the inside, then with spots and blemishes on the outside, until the transformations were complete. He had set his traps, and many were ensnared by his words. After they fully adapted to his rebellious nature, Jubil taught his new followers how to mutate from who they had become, back into the Malachs they had once been.

The transformations were taking place rapidly throughout the kingdom, and word of it began to spread. Jubil's infamous treason was being made known to every Malach in the land. A great upheaval arose and the Malachs began to separate, some continuing in their allegiance to the King, while others were being lured away by Jubil's deception.

Michael and Gabriel appeared before the King, their innocent hearts torn asunder, asking Him how any of their fellow Malachs could succumb to this desire for anarchy, especially Jubil!

The King listened intently as they explained their concerns and fears that maybe the entire kingdom, along with the Zera, would end up as hideous beasts if something wasn't done. Up until this point, the Zera had not heard Jubil's deceitful words, and Michael and Gabriel wanted to keep it that way.

"Lord!" said Michael. "What will happen if the Zera are influenced by Jubil? What will happen if they follow him?"

As Michael pleaded his case before the King, he saw something that concerned him in the King's eyes. Hesitantly, he asked, "Lord, you already know, don't you?"

"Yes, Michael," the King replied. "I do know. It has begun."

"What has begun?" asked Gabriel.

"The rebellion has begun! Jubil has committed the ultimate betrayal, and his heart has been tainted. Because he has desired to be the greatest in this kingdom, his appetite for power has overshadowed his love for me. My heart is burdened for Jubil and those who are following him. I have loved them dearly, and I never wanted this for any of them, but Jubil has made his choice. Alas, he is consumed with evil now, paranoid, and suspicious, leaving no room for hope neither for him nor those he infected."

"Why didn't you stop all of this from happening, my Lord?" asked Michael, anxious yet reverent.

"If I had, would I not be a tyrant?" asked the King. "Would I not be one who forces His will on others? Did I not choose to create you with free will because of my love for you? My hope was that all of you would love me in return!"

"Then what must we do?" asked Michael.

"We have no choice!" said the King, sternly. "Jubil was warned! We must cast him and his followers out!"

The King then put His hands on Michael and Gabriel's shoulders, forming a huddle, and said, "I am afraid war is upon us, the war that I had anticipated, but longed never to see." The King paused for a moment. "War is not good, but it is the only way to cleanse the land. Jubil has chosen to be my enemy. From this day forward, he and his followers will be known as *Rah Malachs*, which simply means *evil Malachs*. We must separate them from that which is good, purging all wickedness."

The King turned to Michael, drew His sword, and laid the tip on Michael's head. Michael knelt before the King and listened.

"Now is your time to shine, Michael. You will defeat Jubil and the Rah Malachs. You are a mighty warrior, but remember don't put your trust in the multitude and the great strength of your horsemen, but in your King, for my strength will be with you. Don't forget, even though your horses have been made ready for the day of battle, your victory rests in me. Go now; find the Rah Malachs."

"Lord, how will I know who is a Rah Malach? I mean, they can disguise themselves perfectly. How will we discern between true friend and foe?"

SEEDS ARE SOWN

The King pointed to Michael's mouth, saying, "Speak my name and the Rah Malachs will turn into hideous beasts before you, thus showing their true identity. When they change, they will flee. They will unite in the forest and prepare for war. There you must face them, but when they are defeated, bring them here for judgment. I have prepared a place for them on the far side of the sea, an empty place void of my presence, bleak and gloomy. There they will experience the full terror of the path they have chosen. In that prison, their evil desires will bring about their own demise. Eternal suffering will be the sentence they have brought on themselves."

"Yes, Lord, I pity them for the path they have chosen. My heart aches for them; still, I will do as you say. Not one of them will go unpunished." So Michael went on his way gathering troops for his mission.

The King then turned to Gabriel and told him to gather his messengers, separating first the ones that have pledged their allegiance to Jubil. "*Most importantly,*" said the King with great emphasis, "make sure that Jubil's words do not reach the Zera. Blow your trumpet, and have them gather here in the courtyard so we can protect them in the palace. Once Michael has Jubil restrained, take the Zera to where I have prepared a beautiful paradise for them. It is only a stones throw away from the prison. It is a place that I call *the garden*. Once they are there, they will be kept from harm by a protective veil that I have placed over it."

"Yes, Lord," Gabriel said. "We will take the Zera there quickly and not one will be lost."

Gabriel made haste and gathered his messengers, watching as some of them turned into hideous beasts when the name King Adonai was spoken. It was difficult for Gabriel to think that even one of his messengers could have fallen for Jubil's lies; nevertheless, he continued doing what the King commanded, making sure that the Zera were contained in the palace until they were ready to be transported to their new home in the garden.

THE KINGDOM DIVIDED

War? Michael pondered as he gathered his troops. Everything was changing so rapidly. *I don't know if I am ready for this. It's hard to imagine harm and pain coming to any of the Malachs, even if they do deserve it. Still, something inside me tells me that everything will work out for the good of those who love the King.*

Michael did as the King told him. Starting with his troops, he proceeded to make sure that none of them had succumbed to Jubil's lies. He spoke the name *King Adonai,* and when he did, the ones who were Rah Malachs changed into hideous creatures before his eyes and fled into the forest. Some had large, bloodshot eyes and horns protruding from their heads. Others had scales or spikes covering their bodies with faces like piranhas, each one seemingly uglier than the one before. Michael was saddened to witness the few of his troops that had fallen into Jubil's web of deceit; still he continued to reveal their identity.

As soon as Jubil found out that the Rah Malachs were hiding in the forest, he went to them and addressed them with his venomous tongue. "You do see what is going on here, don't you?"

The Rah Malachs gave him their full attention.

"The King has found out that we have been enlightened to the truth, and He doesn't like it. He wanted us to continue being His puppets, using us to teach the Zera, only to discard us when He was finished with us. Now, we who are brave enough to make a stand are considered the enemy."

"Enemy?" asked a Rah Malach.

THE KINGDOM DIVIDED

"Yes, enemy," shouted Jubil sternly. "The King sees us as rebels, nonconformists. To Him we are the ones who buck the system. The truth is we are not the ones who are just going to sit back and let Him play us for fools."

The Rah Malachs' shouts and applause were heard throughout the forest. Jubil was building up a spirit of rebellion as he spewed out his false accusations. He told them they needed to prepare for war, for the King would most assuredly attack.

"Why would the King attack us?" one questioned.

"Don't be so naïve!" said Jubil, impatiently. "What do you think you have been training for? Michael has been teaching us to fight. Did you think this was a game? Well it's not a game; this is real! I'm telling you, the King is probably preparing to attack as we speak. So we have to get ready now! There's no time to lose. I want all of you who have swords, bows, armor, and shields to bring them here. Also, we must gather large stones and find some rope. Most importantly, we must decide when to retaliate, and if possible, take them by surprise!"

A Rah Malach spoke up. "I saw Michael and his troops gathering in the meadow between the forest and the palace."

Suddenly, another Rah Malach came running through the forest shouting, "They are planning to take the Zera away."

"What do you mean, take them away? Where are they taking them?" shouted Jubil.

"I heard news that the King is planning for Gabriel and his messengers to take the Zera to a far away place, a hideout called the garden. Michael's troops are assembling in the meadow to protect them as we speak. What are we going to do?"

"Nothing yet!" said Jubil. "We'll let them take the Zera just as they have planned. Right now, we will take time to strategize and prepare. When Gabriel and all the messengers are gone, the odds will be in our favor. That will be the time for us to strike, and strike we will!" Jubil's evil laughter reverberated throughout the forest.

Meantime in the meadow, Michael groped for words of encouragement to speak over his warriors, while warning them of the gravity of the mission. The sport of fighting was tough enough for the Malachs to comprehend; now fighting for real was almost unfathomable, but because of their love for the King and the Zera, they were willing to do their best to fight alongside Michael. Michael boosted the morale of his Malachs by telling them how proud he was of them and assuring them of the King's immeasurable love for them.

"Fear not!" said Michael, "the King's power goes with us, and He who is in us is greater than he who is in the forest. Each one of you is a valiant warrior serving under the King of kings. Today we will triumph over evil, and this kingdom will be safe once again. Fight for honor, fight for integrity, let's fight for the King and His kingdom."

Victorious shouts filled the meadow and overflowed into the palace following Michael's speech.

From the upper balcony of the palace, the King watched all that was taking place. Once Gabriel saw that the troops were in position, he blew his trumpet, and it sounded throughout the kingdom. Every ear could hear it, including Jubil and the Rah Malachs. When Jubil heard it, chills ran up and down his spine, and he was momentarily shaken to the core.

After the horn was blown, the Zera gathered in the King's courtyard. Soon all the messengers began transporting them and their belongings to the garden. The large messengers picked the Zera up in their strong arms, and then, using their great wings, took flight. The smaller messengers gathered the Zeras' belongings and followed behind with wings pumping like little bumblebees trying to keep up. "Hey, wait up!" they hollered with small, squeaky voices.

Michael and his warriors stood guard in the meadow until the last Zera was taken beyond the forest where Jubil and his troops were hiding. After they were out of sight, Michael and his troops came back to the palace. The King stepped out to meet them.

"I can feel it in the air, King Adonai," said Michael. "Jubil is preparing his troops, and they are about to storm the palace. Many of them were fully equipped with swords, bows, and armor, and have been trained to fight. I'm sure they will attack while Gabriel and his messengers are gone. That is when Jubil will think we are at our weakest."

Speaking with His usual sureness, the King said, "You are correct Michael, everything will happen as you have said."

Then Michael, with some concern, said to the King, "Lord, I know that Jubil is very strong and cunning, and that you have given him great power and might. I also know that we do not have the help of Gabriel and his men right now, but I want you to know that those of us who stand before you today will fight bravely and honorably to protect the Zera and this kingdom. We will stand firm in the strength you have given us, and we will do our best to defeat Jubil."

"Do not be afraid," said the King. "I am aware of Jubil's strengths, and I have seen everything he can do, not only in deed, but also with words. He has become very cunning and has caused many to fall away. But remember, Michael, I am on your side, and I believe in you. Jubil and the Rah Malachs are motivated by anger and hatred. You, Michael, are motivated by love. Do not underestimate the power of love. Be strong and courageous, and you shall win this battle. Be on your guard, though, Jubil will not fight honorably. You must watch and listen for his tricks."

After the King spoke, confidence rose up in each of the warriors. You could see the determination building in their eyes. The King then held up a shiny gold necklace with a sparkling gold key hanging from it. Everyone could tell that this was no ordinary key, and that it held a mysterious power. The King motioned for Michael to come close to Him, and then placed the key around his neck.

"Michael, I am giving you the key to the prison where you will take Jubil. This key will open and close the door that binds death inside. When you capture Jubil, after my judgment, take him to the prison and lock him and the Rah Malachs up and throw the key into the depths of the sea."

As Michael picked up the key that was hanging around his neck, he could feel the energy pulsating from it. He looked down at it, asking the King, "Lord, what is death?"

"Death, Michael, is my greatest enemy. Life as you know it is filled with light, happiness, peace, and joy. It is love, relationships, and contentment. Imagine, if you can, what it would be like without all of this, without my presence. That is what death is. Death is darkness, bitterness, and loneliness. It has no peace, no joy, and no color. It's filled with hatred, envy, and regret. It is an endless wandering, a sleepless journey, and a heart that is never comforted. It is torment, restlessness, and hopelessness with no end. Death is a place of weeping and gnashing of teeth." The King looked down as he spoke. "Michael, death, in the simplest terms, is the absence of life."

With that, another tear fell from the King's eye, shaking the ground once again. Jubil, out in the forest, stopped what he was doing and looked toward the palace. Fear gripped him, then, suddenly, was crowded out by the hatred and jealousy that had been brewing there.

The King said, "I regret they have made this choice. I wish there could have been another way."

Michael nodded and said, "Yes, Lord, I agree."

He then turned to the troops and said, "Mount up and prepare for battle; it is time to face the enemy."

Mounting their horses, they headed out to the meadow in preparation for their first war, quickly falling into formation. The swordsmen formed in the front and archers in the rear. Michael was astride a large white stallion positioned in front. The other horsemen lined up on each side of the formation, ready for any flank attack.

Michael raised his sword, and with his horse rearing up, shouted, "For the King and the Zera, we will fight!"

Right then, a loud rumbling sound came from the forest. The sound of limbs snapping, trees cracking, and loud roaring burst through the darkness. The trees began to shake and toss back and forth violently. The ground trembled. Michael's eyes were fixed on Jubil and the Rah Malachs as they pounded through the trees. Michael was repulsed as he caught sight of Jubil. It was the first time that Michael had seen him since the transformation. Jubil was a huge beast, more hideous than all the others, worse than Michael could have imagined. His legs and feet were like that of a swine. His skin was like a serpent's. His hands were like an eagle's talons, eyes like a viper, and face like a dragon with smoke filtering out of his nostrils. He pushed the trees out of his way with his massive strength and plowed through them, as though they were merely tall grass. Jubil was very intimidating, but Michael stood his ground and showed no sign of fear. All of Michael's troops were eager to begin the attack and charge into battle, but Michael held them at bay.

"Steady," yelled Michael as Jubil's army continued toward them. "Hold your formation!"

Michael listened carefully to what sounded like a faint whistling in the air. As he looked into the sky, he noticed that at the top of the trees Jubil's archers had launched thousands of arrows. Jubil's aggressive advance was only a distraction to confuse Michael and his troops. Had Michael charged out to engage in battle, his troops would have been too preoccupied by the fight to notice the barrage of arrows. However, just before the arrows reached them, Michael cried out in a very loud voice, "Cover!"

Immediately, all his troops covered themselves with their shields, and none were injured. Jubil, furious that Michael had foreseen his strategic plan of attack, still proceeded to advance. Michael ordered return fire from his archers, and thousands of arrows were shot up to the trees in a flash. Instantly, many of Jubil's archers fell from their perches.

Michael shouted, "Advance!" and his troops charged toward the enemy with swords drawn.

Of course, Jubil had an alternate plan. As Michael's troops drew closer, Jubil screamed, "Release!"

Just then, large stones catapulted into the sky above the troops. Before the battle began, Jubil had his men stretch some of the trees back until the tops touched the ground and then secured them with ropes. They then placed large rocks on top, only to cut the ropes tossing the boulders up in the air. What Jubil had not considered was that the allegiance of the trees was to the King, and when the ropes were cut, the trees resisted with all their might. The rocks were flung into the air, but fell short of their targets, smashing many of Jubil's own troops. At the same time, many of the trees shook the remaining archers out onto the ground. Jubil was outraged. He had hoped to defeat Michael's troops underhandedly; now he would have to fight them face to face without the aid of his most powerful tool, deception.

At the edge of the tree line, the battle raged with sparks from swords clashing and grunts from Rah Malachs being thrown to the ground. The fighting went on for hours, and Michael and his warriors fought bravely. When Jubil's Rah Malachs saw the strength that Michael and his mighty Malachs possessed, they grew very discouraged and afraid. They had seen all of Jubil's strategies fail, and not one of Michael's troops had been harmed in any way. This caused the Rah Malachs' morale to plummet.

Finally, Jubil's troops were overpowered, and they surrendered; Jubil would not. He quickly flew up into the sky and began to flee above the hilltops. He would have escaped if Michael had not intervened. As Jubil reached the top of the hill, one hundred of Michael's archers stepped out from behind the bushes, launching arrows into the sky. The arrows flew at Jubil with lightning speed and precise accuracy. Each arrow was fastened to a long rope that was tied off on the ground. As arrows began to strike Jubil, he fought to break free, snapping many of the ropes, until finally there were too many for him to resist. Jubil struggled for a while until his strength failed, then finally collapsed to the ground.

At last the battle ended, and a sense of peace fell on the kingdom once again. Michael and his troops bound Jubil and all the

Rah Malachs in the strongest chains and brought them into the courtyard for the King to pronounce His judgment.

As the Rah Malachs stood trembling before the King, He began to speak. With a voice like thunder, He said to Jubil, "You were admired by many Malachs because of the splendor I had given you. You were beautiful, and you trusted in your beauty, allowing yourself to be deceived! In addition to all your wickedness, you lavished your words on others, bringing upon them the same fate I promised you. Now my hand is stretched out against you. Darkness and gloom will be your only friends. Death will be your closest companion."

Then the King turned to Michael and demanded, "Take them away!"

The Rah Malachs were terrified. Jubil, on the contrary, hissed at the King, lashing out at Him, shouting, "This is not the end of me; I will destroy you and your precious Zera!"

The King turned His head in disappointment and pointed toward the prison.

"Take them!" the King commanded. "Take them to the prison where their just reward is waiting for them."

Michael and his troops jerked on the chains aligning the Rah Malachs, causing Jubil to growl. Michael, with his massive strength, grabbed Jubil's chain and tied it around his snout, jerking him into a humbled position. With Jubil's head hung low, he was taken along with the other Rah Malachs down to the sea where large boats awaited them. Immediately, they set sail across the sea to the prison.

It was a long distance to the other side of the sea. Fog began to gather around the ships, creating poor visibility. The waters became rough and treacherous, but after some time, the fog lifted and land appeared before them. They approached the shoreline and saw that the land was dreary and colorless. Rocks and jagged edges covered the ground, and no vegetation grew there at all. The place was desolate, ugly, and lifeless, with thick patches of fog

REMEMBER

hovering over. The boats came to a sudden stop as they beached upon the rocky shore.

Michael and his men unloaded Jubil and the Rah Malachs and led them up the hill to their final destination. Malachs and Rah Malachs alike walked cautiously as they ventured up the unfamiliar crags. At the top of the ridge, they saw a huge wall with a giant gate. The gate was massive in size, over thirty feet tall. It was seven feet thick and made from the strongest iron.

Jubil looked up at the huge gate, realizing that it was the barrier that would soon separate him from life as he knew it. The severity of his punishment was beginning to sink in as he sensed the horror that awaited him. The closer Jubil got, the more he could feel the intensity of the heat and smell the unbearable stench emanating from the prison and its surroundings.

Michael, trying to ignore the smell, passed through the gate and then took the key and unlocked the doors. The doors slowly creaked open. The hinges screeched loudly and then a putrid smelling smoke excreted from the depths of the prison. As it surrounded them, chills riveted Michael's body. This place was more horrible than anything he had expected. Still, Michael pushed forward. Once inside, he locked up each Rah Malach in his own cell. Jubil was taken to the bowels of the prison where he was bound in chains. All the Rah Malachs, except Jubil, cried out, pleading with Michael to spare them from that horrible place. Michael could not; he had to fulfill the orders that the King had given him. Jubil sneered and growled at Michael in disgust; Michael ignored him. When the last Rah Malach was locked in his cell and Michael and his men were outside, they closed the giant doors, slamming them shut with a loud thud. Michael inserted the key in the lock, giving it a turn, causing a loud shriek to fill the air as seven deadbolts engaged in the locked position. Michael shut the gate behind him and walked down to the shoreline, took the key from around his neck, and cast it as far as he could into the depths of the sea. Michael and his troops let out a triumphant shout. Meanwhile, inside the prison, the Rah Malachs continued with their agonizing moans of suffering.

As Michael and his troops rejoiced, the sound was so loud that it echoed through the hillside and reached Gabriel in the garden. Gabriel and his messengers had just completed their task of delivering the children to the garden. When Gabriel heard the rejoicing, he flew in the direction from which it came, and just over the highest hill he saw Michael and his troops. Gabriel drew his trumpet and with a loud victorious blast announced his coming. Michael turned and when he saw that it was Gabriel, he ran up the hill to meet him. Gabriel flew down to Michael, and they hugged one another. Gabriel told Michael that they had safely delivered the Zera and told him about the beauty of the garden.

Then Michael pointed to the prison and said, "You can't imagine how horrid that place is. My heart aches for Jubil and the Rah Malachs, but, like the King said, they have chosen their own fate."

Gabriel agreed, though realizing at the same time just how close the garden and the prison were to each other. *I wonder why the King placed Jubil so close to the Zera.* he thought to himself.

Michael was more concerned about how late it was getting and knew they needed to get back to the kingdom since morning was soon approaching.

"It's getting late, let's gather our troops and head home." Michael conveyed.

"Sounds great," said a relieved Gabriel, succumbing to the idea that the King had everything under control.

Gabriel blew his trumpet. The troops and the messengers gathered and headed homeward.

A HAVEN

The morning dawned with a beautiful sunrise; the sky was painted with rich orange and pink strokes. However, the atmosphere throughout the kingdom was not so bright. A spirit of heaviness hovered over the Malachs as they somberly made their way toward the palace. When they arrived, they met with the King in the courtyard, and the King could easily see that they had troubled hearts. Michael stepped out in front and said, "My King, the Malachs are deeply burdened by all that has happened. I know you told me that it was Jubil's love for power that caused him to rebel, but it is still hard for everyone to accept! Many are asking how Jubil and the others could become so evil."

The King looked over the Malachs gathered in front of him and truly felt their pain, but before He could speak, others cried out from within the crowd.

"Why did some Malachs become evil and not us?"

"Yes, and how do we know that we won't become evil?" asked another.

The King motioned with His hand for them to settle down, then He addressed their many questions and concerns saying, "My heart grieves with all of you. I know this was not easy, but it's over now. I want you to be at peace; for you have nothing to fear. You have been tested and found true, and I am very proud of you."

"When were we tested?" blurted an anonymous voice.

"Well," said the King, "you were all here when Jubil started spreading his detrimental lies, weren't you? By a show of hands, how many of you chose to believe him?"

A HAVEN

Looking around, there were no hands raised.

The King continued. "The reason the others turned away and followed Jubil was because they wanted to believe what he was saying. They did not keep their hearts pure, and so they were deceived. As you can see, you have all remained faithful. You persevered and endured, and I say—well done!"

The Malachs looked at each other with tear-filled eyes, and suddenly a calm soothed their hearts, worry lifted from each of them.

Gabriel stepped forward next to Michael and asked, "Now that Jubil and his Rah Malachs are locked up, should we go and retrieve the Zera from the garden and bring them home?"

The King looked somewhat uneasy, exhaled a deep sigh. "Unfortunately, Gabriel, this is not possible," He said. "The testing may be over for you, but it has just begun for the Zera. From this day forward, we must focus our attention on helping them. I will be visiting them in the garden soon. Before I go, I need to pick our next worship leader. It is very important to have someone leading everyone in worship while I'm away. I need him here in my throne room, filling it with my power continually."

Each Malach looked around curiously, wondering who the King might choose.

The King pointed to Basil, and said, "Please, come; let me anoint you just as I anointed Jubil."

Afterwards, the King asked Michael, Gabriel, and Basil to stay behind while the others turned in for the night. "Tomorrow I will visit the Zera," He said. "Michael, you and Gabriel will accompany me. Basil, you will stay here at the palace with the other Malachs and start each day with worship and my anointing will bring comfort and peace to the kingdom while I am away. You and your musicians are to be steadfast. In the days to come, your gifts will be essential."

So the next day the three of them set off on their journey to the garden. Michael was ecstatic that he was finally going to see the Zera's new home. He had images playing in his head of what the garden might look like based on Gabriel's description, but when they arrived, he found it even more pleasing than he had imagined. As soon as they got out of the boat, he stepped onto the beach. It was snow white and it glistened in the sunlight. Michael kicked off his shoes and felt the sand between his toes. It was silky soft and warm. Up ahead, massive trees bordered the forest. Michael looked up at them in awe. The tops seemed to stretch up to the sky, piercing the clouds. The bases of the trees were so broad that ten Malachs together could not possibly reach their arms around them.

"Now, these are trees," said Michael.

Pressing on, he admired the serene forest with its thick green foliage. There were giant ferns, tall grasses, colorful wildflowers, blue spruces, pine trees, and mighty oaks so large that an entire city could rest in their shade. Spaced evenly below the trees, under their shade, were mushrooms of different shapes and sizes. Moss-covered rocks were scattered here and there. As they strolled along, streams of light burst through the leaves, producing a dazzling laser show. The sound of birds singing and frogs chirping set the show to music. In the opening ahead, was a breathtaking waterfall flowing from a tall mountain. The waterfall splashed into a deep blue spring, and the most brilliantly colored rainbow appeared in its mist. The spring spilled into a quaint little stream that glided calmly through the peaceful garden.

The garden reminded Michael of the kingdom in some ways, but it definitely had its own characteristics and charm. It was quite enchanting and serene... As Michael inhaled, his nostrils were filled with the freshness of the nearby stream, and the aromatic wafts from the assorted orchards and fruit bearing bushes carried in the breeze. You could almost taste the various fruit flavors.

Animals throughout the garden welcomed the three with their own special songs. Birds, lovely and unimaginable in variety, warbled ceaselessly. There were pink flamingos in the water, yellow and blue canaries in the trees. Songbirds of every color covered the branches like ornaments placed neatly there. Beneath the trees, peacocks, turkeys, and pheasants displayed their magnificent tail

A HAVEN

feathers, and beautiful birds of paradise paraded in their splendor. The deer, the tigers, the wolves, the bears, the foxes, along with rabbits, squirrels, and many kinds of furry animals lived together in peace, just like in the kingdom.

The King and the Malach's sight seeing came to an abrupt halt as they were drawn to the sound of pounding and chopping off in the distance. Just around the bend, they saw the Zera busy as beavers, working together in perfect unity. Much like honey bees diligently building their hives, the Zera constructed their homes. Their houses weren't elaborate like back in the kingdom, but they were sufficient for a temporary dwelling. They sang while they worked and seemed to be having a great time. When they noticed the King, they immediately stopped and ran to Him, so very excited to see Him.

"It's the King!" said one of the Zera.

"Father, you're here!" said another.

The Zera gathered around the King in anticipation of what He had to say about the garden—why they were there and when they would be coming home.

"Are we safe now? Are we coming home?" they asked presumptuously.

"Not just yet," said the King. "When the time is right, I will bring you home to live with me forever. This you can count on."

The King, seeing their perplexed faces began to explain. "I have created this garden for you as a temporary dwelling. I want you to make it your home for now. I am giving you complete authority and dominion over it."

One asked, "Why must we live here Father? You created us to be with you in your kingdom, not to be here, away from you."

You could see the sad looks upon their faces as smiles turned to frowns.

The King smiled reassuringly and said, "I will always be with you. Even when you don't see me, I will be there. Do not be afraid, if I am with you, who can be against you. You are my precious jewels, and I have created you for greatness. I formed you in my very image, and though you don't look or feel like it right now, someday you will be just like me."

They looked at each other and then to the King. They felt so small and inferior, wondering how in their wildest dreams, they could ever become like Him?

The King then asked the Zera to take a walk with Him. Strolling along, He continued to share. "I have great plans for you in my kingdom, but before I bring you there, there is much you must learn here. Listen to what I have to tell you—following my instruction will be wisdom for you. Wisdom will be your friend. Find it, and you shall do well. Learn from it, and you shall prosper.

As they walked along, the animals followed close behind.

"The animals will be your companions, take charge of them and care for them. All seed bearing plants will supply food for you, eat any of them you desire for everything is good!"

He then warned them very sternly, saying, "You can live your life freely here in the garden. There is only one thing I forbid!"

Right then He stopped at a clearing at the top of the hill and looked in the direction of the prison. The Zera looked down and saw the prison for the first time. Darkness surrounded it and smoke rose from its foundation. Every eye was watching the King, and every ear was attentive.

He pointed at the clearing just beyond the forest and said, "You are not to go beyond this point! Do not go down in the valley, and whatever you do, do not speak to those inside the prison for any reason. If you do, Jubil will take full advantage and spread his lies in order to destroy you. If you believe Jubil's lies, you will forget your King and then your fate will be the same as his, and you too will surely suffer and die alongside of him."

"Suffer and die?" asked Aaron. Michael and Gabriel bowed their heads.

The King looked upon them with compassion. "Death you have never known. It is unlike anything you have ever experienced. At first it creeps in, bringing oppression, loneliness, bitterness and sorrow; then it's accompanied by sickness and disease, toil and torment. I know this sounds foreign to you, but trust me, you wish never to know it. For death steals your peace, your joy, and all of your color. Your shouts of joy become cries, dancing turns to mourning, and rest to never ending hopelessness. It is a sleepless journey with no end. Heed my words this day!"

The children looked somber.

The King continued. "Some may be wondering why I placed the prison so near to the garden. Let me explain—the Rah Malachs, who are in the prison with Jubil, were loved just the same as you. Despite all the love I had given them, they still made room in their hearts for evil to take root. Jubil was the first to entertain evil, and once he accepted it, he caused it to spread throughout my kingdom. They have done a terrible thing, rebelling against their creator. Now their punishment will be great. They are forever condemned. The worst part of their punishment is that while they are living in that horrible place, they will be able to gaze upon the paradise that I have created for you. They will remember what they once had and what they have now lost."

Soberly, the King said, "The prison was also placed here for you to see. I want it to serve as a reminder of what took place when my servants rebelled. When you think of the prison, you will remember what happened to Jubil. I warned him, yet he did not listen. I could not spare him, nor will I be able to spare you. That was not my plan for him, and neither is it my plan for you. Do not forget that I have good things planned for you, plans to prosper and bless you."

The Zera looked down at the prison, terrified to the core of their being.

"No, Father," some said, shaking their heads from side to side, "we will never forget you. We will never forget your love and mercy, for you are a great King, and you give us good gifts."

The King wanted the impact of His warning to be profound. As they walked back to the waterfall, the King continued to share with them.

"I want you to be fruitful and multiply; occupy this land, take control of it, and cultivate it. Be good stewards of this garden until the day I bring you home. Let one male join with one female to become husband and wife, and when you come together, create for yourselves a family of your own. Teach your family what I have shared with you, and teach them to do the same things that I have told you."

When they reached their destination, the Zera gathered around the King, knowing that He was preparing to return to the kingdom. They did not want the moment to end; they wanted to enjoy the King's presence for just a little longer.

Again, He reminded them that He could see them and hear them from His throne room, and that they should never feel alone. He said that He would visit periodically and that Gabriel and his messengers would come to inspire them to remember everything the King had told them.

Then the King said, "I am leaving now, but soon I shall return."

The Zera waved goodbye as the King and the two Malachs began their journey home.

As they traveled back to the kingdom, the King told Gabriel that he and his messengers were going to be very busy from this point forward. Michael had a look of contentment on his face for he thought his work was finished. He leaned back and glanced at Gabriel with a smirk. Seeing this, the King smiled. "Don't think you're getting off that easy Michael, there is much for you to do as well."

Michael gasped, "What am I training for your Majesty? There is no one left to battle."

Then the King said to him, "Remember when I told the Zera that one day I would bring them home to live with me?"

"Yes," said Michael.

"Well, when that day comes, we will be taking them home in style."

"What do you mean?" asked Michael, curiously.

"When we pick them up, we will be riding on horseback," said the King.

"My Malachs are well trained on horseback."

The King replied, "Not with these horses. These horses will be like none you've seen before. These horses will be able to fly. I am creating them specifically for that day. When that day comes, we will be dressed in our finest armor, riding on the clouds, and shining like the sun. Like I said, we will enter in style, and all eyes will be on us from one end of the horizon to the other."

Michael and Gabriel looked at the King, quite surprised and anxious for that day.

A STRANGE CREATURE

As time passed, Aaron and Eden were the first to marry and have a baby in the garden. They named their son Ryan, and he was the talk of the town. Ryan was as cute as a button. He had his mother's bright green eyes and dark brown hair and his father's broad nose. Everyone was excited about this new addition. It was a miracle to see how this baby grew in Eden's belly and how he was born so small and helpless. He was tiny and weak now, but some day he would be big and strong like the rest of them. Surely this too was a mystery—as if the King was showing them how some day they would grow up to be like Him. Soon after Ryan was born, Eden conceived again and had another son. They named him Jared. Jared was a perfect replica of his father. Both boys grew to be leaders in the community.

Gary and Karen were the next to become husband and wife. Karen was a beautiful, petite, blond-haired female Zera with deep blue eyes. Gary, on the other hand, was a very tall, brawny male Zera with dark hair and a muscular build. He was well known for the strength and skill he possessed. Shortly after they married, Karen gave birth to two golden blonde haired, blue eyed twin boys, Luke and Jake. They grew to be very strong like their father, and they became very popular within the village. Gary was a natural leader and had become a mighty warrior during his training with Michael. Gary taught these skills to his two sons, and soon they too became very skillful in warfare. They worshipped their father and wanted to be just like him.

A STRANGE CREATURE

The King loved seeing the new families grow, and He visited them often. Each time the King came, the women prepared a special meal just for Him. Oh, how the King cherished His time with them. Everything seemed to be going very well in the garden as the Zera multiplied. Very soon, though, and unbeknownst to any of them, circumstances would drastically take a turn for the worse.

One evening after the Zera had been working all day planting crops and vineyards, they decided it was time to relax and spend some time at the waterfall. They swam and played games, ate watermelon, and rested on the banks of the stream.

Meanwhile, down in the prison, an eerie sound came forth from Jubil's cell. He was moaning and thrashing while tugging at his chains, trying desperately to free himself. Jubil couldn't take being imprisoned one more day, and yet this was only the beginning.

"Forever!" said Jubil, choking on his words. "How long is forever? How do you measure eternity? When will I get relief from this torment?"

Jubil's eyes burned into the darkness like fiery embers. Emotions raced through his mind as he tried to pace the floor, yet confined by his chains. The loneliness and emptiness gnawed at him while the unbearable heat was insufferable, all the while, sharp edges of the stony wall tore at his flesh every time he tried to move. For long periods of time, Jubil would fall on the ground weeping and wailing, gnashing his teeth in agony.

Finally he took his mind off his suffering and bridled his emotions so he could think more rationally. *What am I becoming? Am I giving up and letting the King win? No! I'm not giving up. I told the King this was not the end of me, and I will make sure of it.*

Jubil's persistent desire for revenge was fueled by adrenaline. *There has to be a way,* he thought. Then suddenly it came to him. *Wait a minute, what about what the King told the Zera?*

Even though Jubil had been physically locked inside the prison, suffering day and night, he still had moments of time to practice his dark magic. He continued transforming his shape as he had back in the kingdom. Then, stirred by the evil within him, he conjured up ways of bringing fear into those around him. He found that he could project images for others to see, images so real that it would frighten the wits out of the other inmates. Of course, they weren't real, but no one else knew that. Jubil chuckled to himself every time he heard the other cell mates screaming. In time, Jubil realized that he was not only capable of projecting images, but that he was able to see and hear things beyond his cell and the prison walls. In fact, the day the King spoke to the Zera, warning them not to go near the prison, Jubil was listening. He realized that it would be his perfect opportunity to get back at the Zera if he could get them to disobey the King, but how he would accomplish it, he was unsure.

How can I get them to come to the prison? They were warned not to, but if I could get at least one of them to come here, I might be able to get out of this mess, thought Jubil.

Jubil was deep in meditation when something very strange happened. Instead of projecting an image, he began to project himself. It was as if his spirit was stepping outside of his body.

This is amazing, thought Jubil, while looking back at his body bound and chained to the wall. Immediately, he stepped through the wall and ventured outside the prison. In minutes, he leaped into the air and started flying toward the garden. Above the trees Jubil soared, eyes scouring the land, searching, until finally he found the opportunity he was looking for. At the spring where the Zera and animals were enjoying the evening, Jubil noticed a fawn that had wandered a great distance from its parents. Down Jubil dove, enticing the little fawn. Swirling around and around, he managed to lure the young yearling by emitting a sweet aroma of fresh corn and ripe acorns, leading him toward the prison. The fawn had no idea what was taking place; it only knew the smell was irresistible, so up the mountain it went, giving no regard to its surroundings.

As Aaron lay resting on the banks of the stream, he noticed the fawn heading in the direction of the prison. Aaron quickly got up and motioned for Eden to follow him. They noticed the fawn was nearing the top of the mountain.

A STRANGE CREATURE

Aaron was apprehensive to go near the forbidden ground. "Maybe we should wait for it to come back down," he said.

Then Eden said forcefully, "No! We have to go up there; it's just a baby."

Aaron thought about the situation for a moment and then, without any further hesitation, agreed. Both of them set off running up the steep incline. When they reached the top, they separated and quickly began searching the forest edge.

They searched the places farthest away from the clearing first, trying to avoid the area that was off limits, but because of the fawn, they pressed on against their better judgment. Finally, Eden noticed that she had ventured right up to the edge of the clearing where the King had warned them not to go. As she walked along, calling out to the fawn, Eden spotted smoke down in the valley rising up from the prison walls. She didn't want to look, but the temptation was too great. As she gazed down at the filthy, gray prison, she began to tremble. The thought of having to spend eternity there was unimaginable. Eden gulped and then turned away.

As she continued to search for the fawn, out of the corner of her eye, she noticed a strange animal out in the clearing. At first she thought it might be the fawn, but upon closer observation, noticed it was unlike any animal she had ever seen. This creature was strange. Its body was long and slender like a serpent's, yet it had four legs. Its head resembled a lion's, except it had leathery brown skin instead of fur. This animal was so mysterious that it mesmerized Eden. Although intrigued, she noticed that this creature was well beyond the boundaries of the garden, in the forbidden zone, where the King had warned them not to go. Eden knew that it could be in danger, or worse, that it could bring danger to the entire garden.

She called out to it, "Come here, my friend, you shouldn't be out there. It's forbidden."

Then the creature spoke with the strangest voice, soft and alluring, nearly hypnotizing her. It said, "Please, my dear friend, I need your help. I have stumbled into this place, and now I am injured and cannot get out."

Eden started to take a step but then paused. She collected her thoughts and an unsettled feeling erupted in the pit of her stomach., "No! I can't help you." she said. "The King told us never to go out there."

The creature replied with the most compelling voice, "Did the King say that you couldn't come out here if someone needed your help? You can clearly see that I am in need of assistance, so please, will you help me? I don't want to stay here. I'm afraid."

Eden was torn in her decision. She struggled back and forth in her mind, not knowing what to do. She thought again about what the King had told them then exclaimed, "No, I can't! I can't come out there; the King told me not to!"

She ran off into the forest and soon came across Aaron. When she did, Aaron told her that he had found the fawn and sent it back to the garden. Then Eden told Aaron about the creature she had seen in the clearing and how pathetic it looked.

Aaron quickly reminded Eden that the King had warned them not to go near the prison, but Eden, remembering what the creature had said, looked at Aaron and asked, quite convincingly, "Did the King say we couldn't help someone if they were trapped out there? Don't you think the King would want us to help this poor creature? I mean, he did tell us to care for the animals. Which rule is worse to break—going where the King said not to go or leaving that defenseless creature out there alone?"

Aaron stared at his wife, breaking under the pressure of her puppy dog eyes. She continued, "The King is good. Wouldn't it be a good thing to help it?"

Aaron looked down, rubbing his head as if trying to sort things out in his mind. He knew what the King had said, but what Eden was saying made perfect sense too.

"Fine!" he said. "We'll help the creature, but we won't stick around any longer than we have to and while we're there, we won't even look at the prison."

A STRANGE CREATURE

"Okay," said Eden, moving swiftly through the woods, hoping the creature was still doing all right.

Meanwhile, down in the prison, a bit of unexpected joy came over Jubil. He couldn't believe that, not only one, but two of the Zera were coming back. Oh, Jubil was definitely crafty, mentally projecting the creature there for Eden to encounter. It was like a fisherman casting his lure out in front of a fish, working it just right, trying to get the fish to strike. For a moment, he thought that he had lost her. Now he watched, not only Eden returning, but Aaron as well. This was great, two for the price of one.

Once again, Jubil projected the image of the creature just as he had before in the same location. Realizing how well it worked before, he made the image seem even more pitiful. Aaron and Eden arrived at the edge of the clearing right on time.

"There he is!" said Eden. Aaron stopped and looked to where Eden was pointing. He was captivated by the sight of the creature.

"Thank you for coming back, my friend. I knew you would do the right thing."

Suddenly, the creature let out a distressing moan, hoping it would draw Aaron and Eden closer. The sound of it broke their hearts. They looked at each other, their emotions getting the best of them, and then at once they ran toward the creature beyond the clearing. As they entered into the forbidden zone, they expected the worst to happen. Remembering what the King had said, they weren't sure if they would be cast directly into the prison or if some other terrible fate awaited them, but nothing happened; they were still there. "Either the King doesn't see us, or He must understand," said Aaron.

When they reached the creature, they helped him to his feet and led him to safety. They began warning it about the forbidden zone and the penalty for being there. They told it about Jubil's disobedience to the King and how the King had warned them not to go near the prison. Then they told the creature that the King specifically warned them not to listen to anything Jubil had to say.

REMEMBER

The creature responded with the most innocent voice. "Why doesn't the King want you to talk to Jubil?"

"Because he is evil!" said Aaron.

"But how do you know that he is evil?"

"We know, because the King told us he became evil, even his appearance changed to something monstrous," said Eden.

"I see," said the creature, "so you saw this take place yourselves?"

"Not exactly," said Aaron.

"Did you know Jubil?" asked the creature.

"Yes, we all knew him," said Aaron.

"So he was evil when you knew him?"

"No, uh, I mean, yes! The King said he became evil and that's all that matters!" said Aaron—now flustered and frustrated from being put on the spot.

"If you didn't see him turn evil, how do you know the King is telling you the truth? Did you ever think that, just maybe, the King doesn't want you to know something that Jubil knows?"

"No, that's not true!" Aaron said crossly. "The King is good. Jubil is the one who is evil."

"Have you ever spoken with Jubil and heard his side of the story?" asked the creature.

"No, we haven't talked to Jubil, and we never will!" cried Aaron even more angrily.

Eden was nodding her head in agreement.

"Then I guess you'll never know for sure, will you?" said the creature, in one final attempt to cause confusion.

At that, the creature limped off into the woods and disappeared behind a tree. Aaron and Eden were stunned, wondering who this creature was, and why he asked such preposterous questions. They assured each other that what this creature had said was foolishness. They knew the King. They knew that the King was good. This all had to be nonsense. As they headed back to the spring, they turned and looked for the creature one last time; he was nowhere to be found. Eden glanced toward the prison.

DECEIVED

That night Aaron and Eden lay in bed, tormented by the creature's words, replaying them over and over again in their heads. They recalled how Jubil's demeanor was when they lived with him in the kingdom. He seemed noble and honorable. They remembered how well he sang and played music for the King. They didn't remember Jubil being evil; he was always polite. He was a pleasant teacher and friend to both of them, but the King told them that Jubil had transformed into a hideous creature. Of course, they, themselves, didn't see him change, but why would the King say that he did if it wasn't true? The King is good; besides, Michael and Gabriel both confirmed Jubil's transformation. All night, until the wee hours of the morning, Aaron and Eden tossed and turned, thinking about what the King said and then what the creature said.

Eden spoke up first, frustrated and anxious about the matter. "What if the King is hiding something from us? I mean, don't get me wrong, I know the King is good, but what if there is something that He doesn't want us to know?"

Then Aaron, very defensively, snapped back. "What could the King possibly be hiding from us?"

"I don't know," said Eden, "but that creature seemed to know something."

"I know, I know," said Aaron, his confidence shaken, turning toward the wall as if not wanting to think about it anymore.

It was amazing how just a few words could cause such confusion in their thinking. They wrestled in their hearts, until finally they agreed upon what to do to get the answers they so desperately needed.

Aaron looked at Eden, body trembling, sweat beading on his dark forehead. "All right, I have to know the truth. This is driving me crazy. At daybreak we will tell the others that we're going to the spring to dig up some flowers for our garden, and while they are busy working, we'll go to the prison and get Jubil's side of the story."

Eden was afraid, but she agreed with Aaron. As morning dawned, they carried out their plan, making their way to the prison. When they made it to the clearing, they ran down the hill toward the prison as fast as they could. On the way down, they looked to see if the creature was anywhere in sight, but didn't see him. They were focused on getting to the prison, questioning Jubil, and then getting back without anyone knowing they were ever there, including the King, especially the King!

As they approached the prison, the more desolate everything appeared. There was no sign of any life, just dust billowing into the air with every step they took. Entering the gate, the smell of burning sulfur was almost unbearable, causing them to gag. Upon reaching the prison wall, Aaron and Eden started looking for a place to hide. Off to the side of the prison, they saw the perfect spot, a small crevice in the wall that was hidden by a dark shadow.

They both squeezed into the space and then Aaron called out, "Jubil, can you hear me?" A few minutes went by, and he cried out again, this time a little louder, "Jubil, can you hear me?"

Then they heard an old familiar voice, "Who is there?"

"It is Aaron and Eden. We have some questions for you. Can you hear us clearly?"

"Yes, I hear you," said Jubil, sounding somber. "What is it that you wish to know?"

Then Aaron, quick and to the point, said, "We want to hear your side of the story about why you are locked in this prison, but if you choose to lie to us, we will leave. We won't put up with any tricks."

So Jubil spoke ever so gently and comforting, "Yes, I understand; you want to know the truth."

"The truth?" asked Eden, disgruntled. "What truth?"

"The truth about the King," said Jubil. "When I learned what the King had planned for the Zera, I tried to help you. I wanted to warn all of you, but when the King found out, He had me captured, and locked up in this horrible place."

"What the King had planned for us? What do you mean?" asked Aaron, quite perturbed.

"Well," said Jubil, "surely you remember how well I loved and served the King?"

Aaron stood up and peeked through the bars of the window, trying to see Jubil. It was just too dark.

Jubil continued spinning his web of lies. "I never dreamed that the King would do this to us, but look at us now. We are suffering here day and night. You see, Aaron, one day I overheard the King say that His plans for the Zera were not in your best interest. He said things were not working out like He thought, and He was going to have to destroy all of you. So I gathered some of the Malachs to try and stop Him. We fled to the forest to make a plan to do so; that's when the King found out and sent Michael to foil our plans. I knew that the King would lie to you and tell you that I was the one who was evil. It doesn't matter, though, because I know the truth."

Aaron looked at Eden and then again tried to see Jubil. It was still too dark. Then Aaron leaned back against the wall and said angrily, "That is a lie! Why would the King want to destroy us? That doesn't make any sense at all!"

Then Jubil, ever so slyly, spoke again, "The King realized that He made a mistake when He created all of you. He knew that you would be just like Him, maybe too much like Him, and He feared that you would try to overtake His kingdom."

As Jubil spoke, his words enticed Aaron and Eden to believe what he was saying. As they listened, their thoughts became more and more infused with his lies, and Jubil could tell that they were growing weary.

Aaron, with a slight quiver in his voice, asked, "Why would we want to overtake our King?"

"Because it is your nature," said Jubil. "You were created to rule and reign. You are more than conquerors, intended to lead nations. You, Aaron, are the King's offspring, and this is your destiny. The King doesn't want you talking to me because I am your last hope to find out the truth. Now it is up to you to tell the others so they will know as well. Otherwise, you are all doomed!"

Aaron and Eden were in turmoil, trying to keep their wits about them. Then Aaron, very nervously, asked Jubil, "Why didn't the King have the other Malachs throw us in here when He threw all of you in here. And why would Michael and Gabriel lie to us, what would they gain?"

Then, with a convincing voice, Jubil explained, "The King didn't want the other Malachs to know the truth either. Don't you get it? His plan is to make it look like you were the ones who turned evil, just like He did with me. Michael and Gabriel are naïve; they will believe whatever the King tells them."

Eden, feeling very uncertain, interrupted. "I thought they said your appearance changed, that all of you changed into hideous creatures."

Jubil then asked, "Did the King let you see me after this supposed transformation, or did He keep you locked up in His palace?"

"W-w-well," stuttered Eden, "they kept us in the palace until you were blocked off in the forest by Michael, then they flew us directly to the garden."

Finally, Jubil closed the deal, saying, "Then look at me, and see for yourself. Do I look like a hideous creature?"

Both Eden and Aaron rose up on their tiptoes and looked through the window. This time when they looked, they could clearly see that Jubil was as beautiful as they had ever known him to be. He hadn't changed one bit, except for the chains that bound him. When they looked into his eyes, their hearts melted with compassion. They were very baffled, wanting to believe their King, but, because Jubil's words were so seductive, they were finally persuaded.

As soon as they believed, everything inside the prison suddenly became pitch black, except for the bright red glow of Jubil's eyes. A horrid laughter rang from his cell as the whole place began to shake. The tremors were so violent that they were felt throughout the garden and into the kingdom. The Zera stopped what they were doing and looked around, wondering what had happened. The Malachs, in shock, looked toward the sea. The King sat on His throne with His head hanging low, the deed had been done—one of the Zera had disobeyed Him and listened to the lies of the evil one. He knew that this was the beginning of great heartache, and He grieved for His children.

Aaron and Eden were terrified. They had no idea what had just happened. Whatever it was, they knew it wasn't good. They feared that the others would come looking for them and find them at the prison, or, even worse, that the King would find them there. They decided to get home as quickly as possible, and, hopefully, unseen as well.

As they ran toward the garden, Aaron shouted to Eden, "The King will be angry with us if He finds out we've been here. If Jubil is right, He will surely move swiftly to lock us up in the prison."

Aaron and Eden quickly ascended the hill. They were running full blast when they got to the edge of the clearing. As soon as they passed into the forest, they were suddenly slowed down by an invisible force field. They were puzzled, but quickly continued to sneak into the woods before anyone could see them. Now, rather than go home, they decided to go to the spring where they would act as if they, too, were frightened by the tremor.

Aaron and Eden had no idea of what the consequences of their actions would be.

Unfortunately, they were about to find out!

THE CONSEQUENCE

Gary and his boys called for every Zera in the community to gather at the spring so they could assess the damage.

"Was anyone hurt?" asked Gary.

"What just happened?" asked another.

Many were trembling and shaking with fear. Young ones were crying, holding to their parents. Things were chaotic until the leaders finally settled everyone down. Every Zera was accounted for except Aaron and Eden. Ryan and Jared looked worried, then Aaron and Eden appeared out of no where.

Ryan, very concerned, called out to them, "Where have you been? We thought you were getting flowers here at the spring."

Like a child trying to defend his actions, Aaron quickly made up a story, "Well, yesterday we had seen some unusual flowers up on the hill when we were looking for the fawn." This was the first lie ever told in the garden.

Then Eden, agreeing and adding to the lie, said, "Yes, we went up to get them instead of going to the spring. Before we could finish picking them, the ground began to shake. We were frightened so we ran back here as fast as we could, hoping all of you would be here. Does anyone know what happened?"

Ryan, relieved that his parents were safe, said, "Well, I'm glad you're here. You really gave Jared and me a scare." Ryan walked toward his parents, and the crowd began to stir.

"Why don't we call for the King? He will tell us what happened," said one of the Zera.

THE CONSEQUENCE

Aaron and Eden seemed nervous. "Maybe we shouldn't bother the King," they said, fearing for their lives. "Why don't we go check on the animals first?" Aaron and Eden were desperately trying to stall for time so they wouldn't have to be confronted by the King. Now that they were back in the garden, they began to doubt Jubil's words. Their eyes drooped with depression written all over their faces.

Many of the Zera cried out, "King Adonai, King Adonai, where are you King Adonai? Please come and help us!"

A few minutes passed, but the King never appeared. Aaron and Eden were relieved while everyone else was confused. Not knowing what to do, everyone dispersed and headed back to their homes very discouraged. Aaron and Eden walked slowly behind the others.

While walking along, Eden looked down at Aaron's feet, shocked by what she saw. "What's wrong with your feet?" she shouted.

Aaron looked down and noticed that his feet were dull and gray. Frightened by the appearance of them, he looked up at his wife. When he did, he noticed that her eyes were dark gray and sunken back in her head.

He shrieked, then said frantically, "What's wrong with your eyes?"

Eden began to panic. She wanted to look, except she had no way of seeing them without a reflection. Trying to stay calm, she felt them with her hands, but couldn't detect anything by the touch. Eden couldn't imagine her eyes looking anything like Aaron's feet.

She turned back to Aaron and said, "The dust around the prison must have rubbed off on us, we must try to wash it off."

Eden took off running toward the stream with Aaron close on her heels. When they reached the water, they both jumped in and began washing diligently, trying to get rid of the awful discoloration.

"We have to get it off, the others will surely notice!" said Eden.

They rubbed and rubbed, but to no avail. The gray would not wash away. They scrubbed some more, and though the gray was not disappearing, their minds and their hearts were being cleansed by the water. The cloud of confusion from Jubil's words began to vanish from their minds, restoring their thoughts. Suddenly they realized the severity of what they had just done!

"Oh, Father," said Eden, now in tears, "My sweet, sweet King—how could I be so blind? How could I have been so gullible to fall for Jubil's trickery?"

Eden remembered her encounter with the creature and realized that it must have been Jubil speaking through it. Now it all seemed so clear.

Aaron was speechless. Tears fell from his eyes. "What have we done?" he cried with great distress.

Suddenly they heard a voice that sounded like the King's. They hid in the bushes and covered their gray areas, feeling ashamed. It sounded as if the King was standing right in front of them, yet they could not see Him.

They heard His voice again. "Aaron, where are you?"

Aaron looked up and said, "Father, is that you?"

"Yes, Aaron, it is I."

This time they could see Him, but vaguely. It was like seeing Him in a dream. The King was nothing more than an image standing before them. He was there, yet not in bodily form. They had never seen the King this way before. Aaron shook with fear, hiding behind the bushes.

"Why are you hiding?" the King asked. "Have you spoken with Jubil?"

Then Eden spoke up anxiously, "Jubil deceived us, Father. He tricked us into going to the prison, even though you warned us not to."

Then Aaron spoke, "Yes, Father we failed you. We listened to Jubil, and we doubted you. We are so sorry. Please forgive us!"

Each time they said *Father*, the King's heart broke a little more. Holding back tears, the King began to speak, "You know that I love you and never wanted anything bad to happen to you. I chose blessings for you, not cursing. Unfortunately, you did not heed my words! Now you will have to endure the consequences of your actions. At the moment you believed Jubil, when the ground began to shake, the protection of the veil was reversed. You cannot see it yet, but already there are drastic changes taking place. The entire structure has been altered. The power of the veil was designed to keep evil out, but now it is a barrier to keep my power out. This is why I could not come to you in bodily form."

"What are you saying, Father? Why can't you come here?" asked Eden sorrowfully. "I don't understand."

"If I were to come to you in my natural form, the result would be devastating. Not only would the veil be destroyed, but all of you would perish as well. I can't explain everything right now; you will just have to trust me. When the time is right, I will come for you. For now, you will have to live out the remainder of your time in a vulnerable state of existence. Death has entered the garden now, and it will come with a vengeance. It will devour and destroy everything in its path, trying to fill its insatiable appetite. As we speak, the gates to the prison are weakening. Jubil's chains have broken, and he is planning his revenge. He hates you and desires to have you destroyed. You must not give in to him, avoid him at all cost, and do not believe anything he says, for he is the father of all lies!"

"Oh, no!" exclaimed Eden, "if you can't help us, what will become of us?"

"I can help you," said the King, "but you must listen carefully. When you believed Jubil, a door opened, allowing death to enter the garden. Because of this, eyes will be blinded to the truth, and many will be lost. Of course, in the same fashion, when you believe me, another door will open for life to enter, and you can overcome. It will be your choice who to believe. The choice of life and death will always be present before you. Believe me and you will live; believe Jubil and you will die! Go now, and warn the others. Tell them that dark days are coming—tell them their only hope is to remember me and my words. Tell them to listen for my voice, and write down everything I say. Meditate on my words day and night. Teach your children and your children's children so they too will know the truth. Tell them, when the time is right I will come back for them."

The King was looking toward the prison when the ground suddenly began to shake again.

"Go," He said. "Warn the others, and never forget what I told you. Watch for the signs of my coming, resist the words of Jubil, and hang on until I come for you."

As the King spoke those final words, He began to dissipate into the air, as did His words.

"Remember, remember, remember," He said softer and softer. Then, suddenly, the sound of His voice was gone.

Aaron and Eden gripped each other in fear. The reality of what was about to take place would be forever fresh in their minds. They didn't want to move, but they knew they had to warn the others before it was too late. Off in the distance above the prison, the sky began to turn blood red. Dark clouds formed, lightning struck, and thunder roared from the clouds. Wasting no time, Aaron and Eden darted to tell the others.

"This is our fault," Aaron said to Eden, regretfully. "We've gotten everyone into this mess, and today I vow that we will do our best to help everyone get out."

When they reached the village, everyone was huddled close together, shuddering from the appearance of the dark sky.

"What's going on?" someone shrieked.

"Where's the King, and why isn't He helping us?" a quivering voice said.

Like children watching a frightening thunderstorm for the first time, they were consumed with overwhelming terror. They didn't know what to do or where to turn.

When Aaron saw them, he cried out in a loud voice, "Listen to me everyone!"

THE CONSEQUENCE

Gary and Ryan tried to quiet everyone so they could hear Aaron.

Once quieted, Aaron began to speak. "The King has appeared to Eden and I. There is something we must confess."

Every eye was on them.

"We know why the ground shook."

Mouths dropped open.

"Eden and I have gone to the prison."

Everyone was shocked.

Aaron continued in tears, feeling terrible about what they had done. He told them how powerful Jubil's words were and how easily he and his wife had been deceived by the creature.

"The prison has been shaken to its foundation. Death and judgment that were intended for the Rah Malachs have escaped from the prison and are now heading this way. Times ahead are going to be bleak."

Every ear was attentive as Aaron explained the coming torrent. Each of them just stared at him like deer caught in a bright light. They had no idea what to say, and Aaron could see their discomfort. His eyes were filled with sorrow as he looked at them and pleaded for their forgiveness. Then he finished.

"No matter how dark it gets, no matter how bad it seems, just remember the King, and never forget His words! It's our only hope!"

After Aaron confessed, the Zera watched as the storm continued brewing over the prison in the distance. The power of evil grew there, and the chains that bound the Rah Malachs continued to break. When the last chain broke, the Rah Malachs gathered before the massive prison door. The seven locks were still secure, although Jubil knew they were growing weaker by the minute.

"Soon we will be free," said Jubil to all those gathered around. "The time is drawing near for us to take our revenge!" Jubil laughed contentiously and then asked, "What is it that is dearest to the King's heart? What is it that the King treasures more than anything?"

The Rah Malachs looked at each other and evil grins spread across their faces.

"The Zera," one responded.

"Yes!" said Jubil. "That's right. That's what He loves and cherishes the most. The way I see it, if we really want to get even with the King, we will have to destroy the Zera."

"How are we going to destroy them? Aren't they made in the image of the King?" asked one of the Rah Malachs.

"It will be easy," shouted Jubil. "Aaron and Eden have already disobeyed the King. Can't you see? They have freed us from this wretched place and brought our curse upon themselves. The King's anger and wrath that were meant for us now will be released on them. The King Himself said they would surely die if they listened to my words. He said they would share my fate if they disobeyed Him."

Jubil, gloating, continued. "Let me clarify one thing—the King is right to say that they will die, but the King is wrong to think they will share my fate. Instead, they will take my place; in fact, when we're finished with them, they will wish they had never been created." Jubil laughed triumphantly as they waited on the doors to open.

Back at the kingdom, the King explained to the inquisitive Malachs what was happening in the garden, pools of sorrow filling His eyes. "The storm gathers and the sleeping serpent of death awakens. Soon darkness will cover the face of the garden. Zera will turn against Zera, fathers against sons, and sons against fathers. Like a shadow follows a Zera, so will destruction follow them all the days of their lives. Their trials and tribulations will be great. There will be fighting, wars, sickness, disease, and so much heartache."

The King, now staring in the direction of the garden, continued speaking. "In a short time, Jubil and the Rah Malachs will be free to roam in and out of the garden as they please. Like a roaring lion, each will seek out whomever they can devour. They will spread their propaganda like a plague, and many of the Zera will eventually turn away; they will forget their King."

THE CONSEQUENCE

"No, Your Highness, this cannot be!" said Gabriel desperately.

"No!" shouted Michael. "I will defend the Zera to the end. I will take my warriors and defeat Jubil once again. Then we will lock him back in the prison, or at your command, we will destroy him and all of the Rah Malachs once and for all."

Then Gabriel chimed in. "Yes, Lord, and I will take my messengers, and we will stand guard around the garden, protecting the Zera from these horrible events."

The King, feeling great anguish for the Zera, sat silent for a moment, then He mustered up a smile and said, "You are faithful servants. That is why I have chosen you. I know both of you would fight for the Zera. I know you would do anything you could to help them, but the time to fight is not now."

Over the prison, the sky went from blood red to dark gray. Storms began to rage. Thunder bellowed through the valley; hail the size of softballs fell out of the sky, and the wind began to blow violently. As everyone watched from the garden, they could see the sky darkening, lightning flashing, and dark whirlwinds forming in the clouds. They had no idea what to expect, but knew it was not going to be good. Outside the prison, the storm concentrated in a small area above the roof. Tighter and tighter it wound together; then, with a blast, the energy condensed into one place. There was a great rumbling sound, until suddenly, with a loud crash, the force of the storm fell upon the prison. Seven loud explosions were heard as each lock burst into pieces. The door began to creak open ever so slightly. Jubil and the Rah Malachs stood there watching, excited to see what lie on the other side. Immediately, the light from the garden pierced the darkness, and the Rah Malachs were momentarily blinded. They hid their eyes, covering them with their hands, only able to peek out between their fingers. It had been so long since they had seen any light, and it was hard for their eyes to adjust.

In the garden, a sweet, young girl tugged on her mother's dress. Frightened and whimpering she asked, "What is that mother? Why does everyone look so frightened? Are we going to be all right, mother?"

Her mother looked down at her. While trying to hide the tears in her eyes and forcing a smile, she put her hand on her little girl's shoulder and said, "Yes, Sarah, everything will be all right; you must believe that. Everything will be just fine." At that, she pulled her little girl tight to her side and looked back toward the prison, apprehensively waiting the outcome.

DARKNESS SPREADS

Darkness began flowing from the prison throughout the garden. It was like molten lava spewing from a volcano, burning everything in its path. As it crept in, each area it touched changed from bright and colorful to dark gray, dusty, and dull. Flowers and grass shriveled up and died. Trees withered, lost their leaves, and dried up at the root. The crystal clear stream became murky with sludge pouring in from the banks. Life, as the Zera knew it, was disappearing before their very eyes.

Although the King and the messengers could no longer physically come to the garden, they continued to speak to the Zera. In mysterious ways the King would speak to them. To one He spoke through a burning bush, high on a hill top. He gave him ten simple rules for the Zera to follow to protect them from the darkness. The first and foremost was to remember the King. To others, the King spoke through the wind or through the storms giving each of them another nugget to help save them from destruction. In obedience, the Zera expeditiously wrote down everything they heard and everything they remembered about the King and the kingdom. They assembled the writings into a book and called it *The Book of Remembrance*.

• • • • • • • • • •

It had only been a few short months since Jubil and the Rah Malachs were freed from the prison, and already the memory of the King was fading, with darkness stealing it away. Some of the Zera gathered along the seashore at the perimeter of the veil and listened to hear the voice of their King. Karen was one who especially loved to hear His words, vowing that she would never forget Him. She would rise early in the morning to find a quiet place so she could listen as the messengers spoke of their King and of the kingdom from which they came. Sometimes she could hear Basil and the worshippers singing and dancing over her, and Karen would dance and sing along with them. Day after day she tried with all her might to remember, but no matter how hard she tried, the darkness continued to steal her memories. The more they faded, the more difficult it became to retain her true identity. If not for the *Book*, all would have been lost.

Even though the recollection of the King was diminishing, the threat of Jubil was ever present. Every day the Zera prepared for and awaited Jubil's attack. They knew he was free, and they figured it was only a matter of time before he would come to destroy them. Gary initiated training, and chose his two sons, Luke and Jake, to lead separate groups to patrol the perimeters of the garden. Some soldiers were placed in tall trees with horns so that they could sound the alarm at the first sight of the enemy. At night, troops would stand shifts guarding the village so everyone else could sleep peacefully.

Aaron and Eden taught the Zera how to resist Jubil's lies and also about the different tricks he might use. Of course, they knew from experience that his words could be mightier than the sword, and that he was as clever as a fox. They knew that Jubil could deceive the wisest of them, and they hoped that the Zera would not make the same mistakes that they had.

Down in the dark prison, Jubil waited patiently. The Rah Malachs, on the other hand, kept asking him why they weren't training for battle.

"Are you so simple?" asked Jubil. "Do you really think I am going into battle with sword and bow against the Zera? Do you know what would happen if we stir up the King's power within them? Will I wake the sleeping giant? I think not! I have a better plan. The Zera won't be battling against flesh and blood. Their

DARKNESS SPREADS

battle will be with an invisible opponent, against principalities and powers of darkness. Their minds will be the battlefield, and words and thoughts will be their enemy. Look at them; they are already forgetting their King and becoming discouraged. Soon they will forget about their battle with us and start fighting amongst themselves."

Jubil, quite satisfied with his endeavors, said, "I enjoy watching the Zera train. Soon they will be using all that experience to fight for me. Not only that, one day they will serve me as their King. Don't you see? Before this is finished, we will rise up to fight against the King Himself. When this happens, together we will take over His kingdom. I will sit on the King's throne, and all will fall down and worship me." Jubil let out a blood curdling laugh, so sure of his destiny. "We will be patient for now and watch, watch as they grow weary and tired of preparing for a battle that will never happen. Then, when they are worn down, at their lowest point, we will speak to their fatigued minds."

The Rah Malachs listened as Jubil unfolded his dastardly plans.

One of them spoke up and said, "I see it now. Not only will we destroy the Zera in the end, and take back what they stole from us, but we will also use them to work and fight for us in the meantime. We will turn them against each other and then turn them against the King. Imagine the King's face when He sees the Zera bursting into His kingdom to conquer Him. Perfect, perfect, perfect!"

Jubil, pleased that someone was finally getting the picture, told them, "Now you can prepare for battle not with sword, but with tongue, for soon the verbal attack will begin."

As the dark mist crept across the land, animals instinctively moved out of its path. They avoided it whenever possible and feared it as if it was death itself. Eventually, the green areas became more and more scarce. The darkness was taking over, leaving desolation in its place.

Aaron and Eden watched how all the animals were being affected by the invasion. Once the animals were touched by the mist, they would almost immediately become aggressive toward

REMEMBER

one another. Animals that once lived in peace and harmony were now fighting for dominance. Soon only the strong could survive, while the weaker were slain. Aaron and Eden were sickened. Guilt and condemnation plagued their minds as they viewed the dreadful sight of dead carcasses lying out in the fields.

The Zera were being affected by the darkness in the same way. Life became chaotic as the dark fog engulfed the villages. Families and households began to fall apart and dismantle. Pressure and fear weighed down on everyone. The presence of the Rah Malachs made it even worse.

"Where are you going?" cried Karen as Gary and his boys headed out toward the forest.

"We're going to train today. Can't you see the present threat of Jubil and his Rah Malachs?"

Karen looked up and saw Rah Malachs soaring high in the sky like vultures looking down at their soon-to-be meals. "I see them," said Karen, "but we haven't read from the *Book* in days. Surely you remember what we were taught. The *Book* is our only true defense."

"I know that," grumbled Gary. "I heard what Aaron said. I also see the Rah Malachs day in and day out hovering over us, waiting for a time to attack, and I see the land wasting away. Food is becoming more and more scarce. Do you want to tell me how that *Book* is going to change our predicament? Will reading it build a wall of protection around us? Will it put food on our table? I don't think so. Up until now that *Book* has done nothing except remind us of a King who has long since forgotten us. Listen to me, Karen, if we are going to be protected and cared for, we will have to do it ourselves."

"No!" said Karen anguished. "You can't mean that?" Karen cupped her cheeks with her hands, tears welled up in her eyes as her mouth hung open and her lips quivered. "Please, tell me, Gary, you haven't forgotten our King, have you? Tell me that you haven't forgotten our creator?"

DARKNESS SPREADS

"I don't know what I remember anymore. I don't know what I believe either," yelled Gary as he and his boys stomped off into the forest to train.

Karen wept while looking out toward the kingdom. "How long, King Adonai, how long? My tears have been my food day and night. I don't know how much longer I can survive."

From the prison, the Rah Malachs ventured out and hid in dark places close to the garden's edge, observing the Zera while waiting for the right time to attack. Many of them were becoming impatient and restless.

"When Jubil? When will we attack?" asked one of the Rah Malachs.

"Soon," snarled Jubil. "Soon, they will wear themselves out, then we will move in. For now, we will watch and wait."

As the Rah Malachs found their place in crevices, trees, or soaring in the sky, keeping an eye out on the Zera, Jubil constantly searched for something near the sea. The Rah Malachs watched him night after night, wondering what he was searching for. Jubil was the only one who knew about the key that Michael had tossed into the depths of the sea. He knew the key had special powers, and knew that if he could get his hands on it, then, maybe, somehow it could help him achieve the victory he so desperately sought.

After searching everywhere for the key, Jubil was about to give up, until one night he noticed one of the Rah Malachs playing with something. It caught his eye because it was the only thing around that was still shiny.

As he approached the Rah Malach, he asked him, "What is it that you are playing with, my friend?"

The Rah Malach looked up at Jubil and said, "I don't know; look how shiny it is."

Jubil snatched it from his hand and growled. "Where did you find this? I have been searching everywhere for it."

The Rah Malach drew back from Jubil, leery of his response, and replied, "I was climbing a tree near the garden to spy on the Zera when I noticed something shiny in the sea, so I swam down and picked it up. I think it holds some kind of special power. Can I have it back now?"

Jubil turned around, sporting a look that made the Rah Malach weak-kneed and faint-hearted. Then he snarled at him and shouted, "No, you can't have it back! It's mine—all mine! Now I hold its power in my hands, and the King and the Zera will pay."

Jubil held up the key and continued to bellow. "Yes, it is I who will be the greatest."

As Jubil held up the key, he began to change before the Rah Malach's eyes. His power grew, and his form grew with it. With the power of the key, Jubil became even more hideous and gruesome than before. Soon all of them feared him, and in no way would any of them dare defy his commands.

Day after day, Jubil studied the key, determined to find its secret. Whenever he would speak, the key would glow, and soon he realized that it empowered the tongue of its user.

"Oh yes! This is better than I thought!" exclaimed Jubil. "Now I will surely be able to defeat the Zera."

As time passed, the Zera began to let their guard down just as Jubil predicted. Their training nearly ceased, and talk of war was seldom mentioned. The time was right for Jubil and his Rah Malachs to unleash their fury using a bombardment of negative propaganda.

The war began with verbal assaults. First, at night, secretly, they whispered their lies. In time, they gained the Zera's trust by deceitfully befriending them. Then in broad daylight, Jubil and the Rah Malachs wandered about speaking openly. Once Jubil and the Rah Malachs spread their vile words, contentious feelings began to rise up within the Zera. It was ever so subtle at first—a person here and there— then turbulence began to escalate. Each morning when they awoke, feelings like jealousy and strife devoured them. Jubil knew that his words were powerful, and he knew that they would be hard for the Zera to resist. He watched as they began fighting amongst themselves. It wasn't long before they were separating because of the way they talked, or the way they looked, or even because of the color of their skin. He loved to watch them be hateful to one another and see all the hurt they inflicted.

The King grieved in His heart, watching the Zera become deceived so easily. He had warned them in advance and gave them His words so they could be prepared to fight against Jubil, but the darkness made Jubil's words easier to believe than the King's. The King's messengers worked overtime night and day, trying to speak His truth to the Zera, but to no avail. The more the Zera entertained Jubil's negative words, the more darkness spread throughout their minds. A few Zera tried to hold on to their belief in the King as long as they could. Karen, Lyric, and Eden would listen as closely as they could down by the sea. A few of the male Zera appeared every once in a while with them. Soon, even they could not hear the words of the messengers. They knew they were there; they just couldn't hear them any more. Many of the leaders lost their belief in the King, including Gary and his boys. Tensions rose throughout the garden and Karen, along with Aaron, Eden, and their family, were very worried.

Each morning Ryan and Jared would try helping their parents by bringing everyone they could together to read from *The Book of Remembrance*. But, relentlessly, the darkness overwhelmed the minds of the Zera so that they couldn't even remember the King when the *Book* was read. Instead of being one happy family, many had become strangers.

Back in the kingdom, there was a great silence in the land.

"Oh, what a horrible thing this is," said Gabriel, while weeping. "If things continue as they are, the Zera will be no more."

"I know," said Michael. "Their only hope was to remember the King; now all hope seems lost."

Michael and Gabriel looked back at the King who was intently watching the Zera. They wondered what He was pondering.

NO OTHER WAY

Quite some time had passed since darkness consumed the land. The entire garden had become a wasteland of lost memories and broken relationships. A tangible blanket of oppression fell upon and covered the entire land like a thick fog. The animals that survived could no longer communicate with the Zera and feared their very presence. Before long, what was once friend was now foe. Animals had become food.

The Zera became self-indulgent, loving only themselves. Each one was only concerned with his own individual problems and affairs. Work had changed from being fun and gratifying, to hard and mundane. What was once a beautiful garden with a wonderful family had now become an ugly, desolate land filled with bitter and angry people. Even the days were dark and gloomy. Thick storm clouds hung overhead as a reminder of their pitiful condition.

Because of great fear, confusion, and disillusionment, many of the Zera began serving Jubil. Jubil warned any who would resist him against doing so, but Aaron and Eden were not afraid of his threats. They were determined to see him fail in his efforts. Even though the King had long forgiven them, they still felt responsible for the destruction of the garden, and they had vowed to fight, no matter how endless the battle seemed.

Jubil watched as they disobeyed his command. "They will pay for what they are doing, but right now I have other fish to fry." said Jubil.

Jubil's immediate goal was to recruit Gary and his boys as commanders of his army. So, like a hunter selecting the perfect bait for the trap, Jubil thought about the precise words to use to lure them. Finally, without delay, Jubil met with Gary and his sons high on the hill overlooking the garden. Jubil had prepared a picnic filled with the finest of everything to eat and drink. After eating, Jubil reached into a case and retrieved his violin. He began to serenade Gary and his boys, erasing all memories of the King and of the garden as it was before darkness consumed it.

"Look at this place," said Jubil, pretending to be saddened by what he saw. "You may not be able to remember, but this used to be a beautiful paradise."

Gary and his boys looked out over the valley, trying to remember if it ever looked any different; they couldn't recall it being any other way.

Jubil, certain that they no longer remembered, boldly pitched his line before them. "I admire you three. You truly are great leaders and mighty warriors. I'm sure you have heard by now that the Zera want me to be their king?"

"No, we didn't know that," said Gary.

"Well," said Jubil putting his arm around Gary, "the Zera know that I have the ability to clean up this place and restore its beauty. They know that I am one of the few who can remember how things used to be before this *Book* came along."

Troubled, Gary asked, "What book?"

"You know – *The Book of Remembrance*. I believe your wife reads one?"

"Oh, that *Book*," said Gary, wondering how that could possibly be a problem.

"Yes, that *Book* is the cause of all the problems you see now. We used to all work together as a team before that *Book* came along. Who would have thought that a book of wild tales could have changed everyone's ideas so much? It did though. It has caused divisions among us, along with fighting, starvation, and pestilence in the garden."

Jubil's words flowed as smooth as silk from his lips. "I have a vision of seeing this place beautiful once again, like it used to be.

This dream could soon become a reality if I could organize the Zera into cooperating. That is where you come in Gary. I need leaders like you and your boys to help me with my vision. I want you to be my right-hand man. Along with your boys, you can help me see all of this come to fruition. Think about the future of your grandchildren and their children to come. Is this the environment you want them to grow up in?"

Jubil's words pricked the heart of Gary and his two sons. They could imagine clear streams and bright colors throughout the land as Jubil painted pictures in their minds.

"I'm in!" shouted Gary.

"We are too!" said Luke and Jake.

Jubil could see that they were sincerely convinced. He was like a snake charming its victim before the strike.

"Go tell the Zera that I will be their king. Speak of our vision and persuade them about the evils of the *Book*."

Gary and his boys were very proud to serve Jubil. He made them feel like they were a part of something important. Gary quickly became excited about Jubil's vision; but unfortunately, this caused great friction to arise at home. Whenever they brought up the evils of the *Book*, Karen would become irate.

The *Book* was the only plumb line the Zera had to tell right from wrong, and Karen was one of the few who still remembered that it was good and that Jubil was evil. She didn't know the true King anymore, nor could she hear His voice, but she knew enough to know that Jubil was not the one she read about in the *Book*. Karen tried to speak truth to her family, but Gary would not listen. Before long he became so blinded by his allegiance to Jubil that he decided to leave Karen. He couldn't change her and in his mind, she was a rebellious hindrance to the future of the garden.

Karen became very depressed and drifted deeper into the darkness. She gave up reading the *Book* and started becoming like everyone else. At the same time, Jubil had learned a dark secret about the key. Not only did it empower his words, upon closer observation, he found that with the key he could harness the power of death, in all its forms. Jubil quickly took advantage of the opportunity. While holding the key and donning a wicked grin, he spoke into the air and inflicted Karen with a disease that caused her to become crippled. It wasn't long before she lost everything, becoming a beggar in the streets. She was the first of her kind. In the beginning, everyone felt sorry for her, but soon everyone avoided her like a plague. Even Luke and Jake had no trouble ignoring their mother when they passed her in the street.

Aaron and Eden pressed on reading aloud from the *Book* to anyone who would listen teaching and admonishing them. The loss of Karen affected the success of their mission; still, they would not stop. Jubil was getting sick of hearing them read about the King. Even though few people were listening to them, he knew that their reading from the *Book* was holding up progress. He decided that it was time to silence them once and for all, and to do it, he would use the Zera.

Why not? thought Jubil. *Why not put the Zera's training to use? They trained for battle so why shouldn't they try it out?* Holding up the key once again, Jubil spitefully spoke words of Aaron and Eden's ultimate demise.

The next day Jubil sent his Rah Malachs to the place where the few gathered to hear Aaron and Eden read from *The Book of Remembrance*. The Rah Malachs began speaking negative about Aaron and Eden before they arrived. They told the Zera that Aaron and Eden and the *Book* were the cause of all their problems. One of the Rah Malachs said to them, "Can't you see that they are trying to make you believe in something that is not even true, in a king that doesn't exist. They are causing division while Jubil is trying to bring unity. Can't you see the harm they are causing. You need to stop them, stop them from bringing more misery to you and your children."

The Rah Malachs went back to the prison, feeling convinced they had said enough to the Zera to cause ill feelings toward Aaron and Eden. By the time Aaron and Eden arrived, the Zera were worked up into frenzy. The rage radiated from them like heat emitted from a fire, but Aaron and Eden were not intimidated. They continued, as planned, to share the message they had read the night before.

Aaron and Eden spoke boldly to the group, even though no one listened. The Zera covered their ears and yelled derogatory words at them. As Aaron and Eden continued to speak, the Zera gathered around them and drew their swords, shouting and telling them to keep quiet. No Zera had ever hurt anyone physically before, but these Zera looked dangerous, as if some evil force was controlling them. Both Aaron and Eden felt fear come over them. They were tempted to stop speaking about the King, but because it was the Zera's only hope, out of a great sacrificial love, they continued to do so.

Jubil watched from a distance, thinking, *What a joyful sight,* as the Zera grew more and more violent.

Once again, Jubil held up the key and spoke into the air, "Death be upon you both."

Then it happened. The Zera, filled with violent hostility, coerced by Jubil's dark powers, swung their swords. Aaron and Eden fell dead before them.

Jubil smiled.

At that moment, the Zera stopped and dropped their swords, looking with dismay at what they had just done. They had never witnessed such tragedy before. The two bodies lay there lifeless, blood flowing out of them. None of the Zera had ever seen a person die. They didn't know what was happening, so everyone panicked, wondering what to do. They nudged Aaron and Eden to try and wake them, but they couldn't. Death had truly shown its ugly head.

"What have we done?" one of them said.

"Why don't they wake up?" said another.

Finally, one of them felt Aaron's chest and said remorsefully, "Their hearts are not beating. Maybe they are not going to wake up. What are we to do?"

The Zera looked at one another, terrified. They paced back and forth, nauseated and with pale faces. They knew this was really bad, unlike anything they had ever experienced in the garden. After much worrying and fear of what the others might do to them when they saw the horrible act they had committed, they decided to hide the bodies. Still trembling, they dragged the corpses down to the edge of the sea and tossed them into the water, hoping that no one would ever see them again. As they watched, the bodies floated off into the sea and eventually sank to the murky bottom.

The King, watching from His throne room, was greatly distressed from what He had witnessed. The King loved the Zera, and it hurt Him deeply to see them continue down the wrong path.

"The curse has devoured the garden," said the King. "Those who dwell in it are desolate. The joy of the harp ceases."

• • • • • • • • • • •

Since the death of Aaron and Eden, violence, now accompanied by death, had razed the land like a wildfire. Fighting escalated into fierce wars. The cry of Zera dying off in the distance was now a common sound. It was also a familiar sight to see the remains of lifeless bodies spread across the land. The times were grim and the Zera ruthless, each one in pursuit of their own indulgences.

Jubil gloated as he watched the Zera fighting and killing each other. He loved to hear the mourning of families who had lost a loved one, and enjoyed watching all the lame and crippled who had been injured in war. He especially enjoyed how everyone blamed a king they couldn't even remember. Jubil mused that inflicting Karen with sickness added a nice touch. So now he decided to turn up the heat a little bit for the rest of the Zera.

Jubil said, "Karen shouldn't be alone with her disease."

He held up his key and then shouted vile words into the air. "Sickness and disease be upon you all."

At that, he let out a heinous laugh as he watched another dark mist of smoke begin to swirl before him. It grew larger and larger, and then while holding the key tightly in his hand, he blew at the dark mist, causing it to move in the direction of the Zera.

REMEMBER

Each of the Rah Malachs watched as the dark mist passed by and headed toward the garden. Joy came over their sick, demented minds as they imagined the suffering that it would bring on the Zera. Wars and fighting, killing and stealing, and now sickness and disease began to encroach upon their land. The wrath of viruses was merciless. It had no preference as to whom it destroyed. It didn't matter if the Zera were good or evil, young, old, rich, or poor; many were affected. Gloom and despair filled the land, hastening the death of many.

The Malachs watched and wondered if times could get any worse; Michael and Gabriel were very afraid. The King reassured both of them that good would ultimately prevail over evil.

"I have seen their suffering and heard their cries." said the King. "Don't think that one of my Zera has fallen by the sword or suffered with pain, sickness, and disease without me noticing. Just as a mother suffers through childbirth because she knows the reward that awaits her, so my children will suffer—but not in vain, for those that endure will be rewarded."

"Those that endure?" asked Gabriel. "Who can endure? All of them, like sheep, have gone astray. None of them seek you any more; they have all become corrupt and done abominable things."

With fire in His eyes and the voice of a lion, the King said, "It is not finished yet! The battle has only begun. Therefore, do not lose heart. Though outwardly they seem to be wasting away, inwardly they are being renewed, for their momentary troubles are achieving for them an eternal glory that far outweighs it all. So fix your attention, not on what is seen, but on what is unseen. For what is seen is temporary and what is unseen is eternal."

Gabriel looked up to the King and said, "Yes, Lord, we know you have said that everything will work out for the good of those who love you. We have seen your power at work in the Zera, strengthening them and giving them favor when the odds were against them. We know that your power and your words are far greater than Jubil's. Yet we fear, in the end, none of them will believe you, and all of them will serve Jubil and be destroyed."

Then the King reiterated what He had said. "Let me remind you, Gabriel, do not be deceived by what you see, and do not be dismayed by what you observe. What you see with your eyes can diminish what you believe in your heart if you let it. I want you to walk by faith not by sight. Remember, any one of the Zera with my power in them is greater than all of those on the side of evil combined. Know that not one of my children will be destroyed by Jubil, nor join him in his destruction and in his fate."

"What about all of those who have turned away? Will they be saved from Jubil?" asked Michael.

Then the King stated in a firm voice, "Those who believe—they are my children."

Gabriel and Michael both looked confused. They wondered how only those who believed could be the King's children.

Michael said, "My Lord, shouldn't we act quickly then? Shouldn't we go to the Zera now and save them before they are no more? Jubil is cunning, and his tactics have been very successful. If we don't act now, I fear that you won't have any family left to save."

The King smiled. "Are you also so easily moved by what you see? Apparently you still underestimate your King. You are correct in saying that Jubil is crafty. Crafty he is, but wise he is not, for what I have planned for him will completely take him by surprise."

"What is it?" Gabriel asked, as both Malachs became attentive, eager to hear the King's plan of salvation, both hoping they would be involved.

But as the King began speaking, they soon realized that they were not a part of his His plan at all. His plan would involve Him alone.

The King revealed that He was going into the garden to unravel Jubil's lies and restore the Zera, for they had been oppressed long enough. He was not only going to heal them, but destroy the power of death and darkness, thus allowing light back into the land. Both Michael and Gabriel were excited about the King's decision; they pictured him bursting through the veil of darkness, bringing light and healing into the garden.

Michael spoke up. "Lord, shall I prepare the grandest stallion?"

Then Gabriel said with childlike joy, "Yes, Your Majesty. Shall I get ready to blow the trumpet to announce your arrival?"

"No," the King replied. "That will not be part of my plan, just yet."

"What do you mean?" asked Michael. "How do you plan to enter the garden if not as a valiant King?"

"Not like you think," said King Adonai.

Michael and Gabriel, quite bewildered asked, "How then, Lord?"

The King explained, "As I mentioned before, I cannot go there and readily change their circumstances. It's not that I don't have the power to do so, it's just that if I did, the outcome would be disastrous for the Zera. Were I to burst into their world with all my power, it would surely destroy everything in the garden. If I were to bring my Zera home without them reaching maturity, they would all be lost. My plan is to go to them not as their king but as a servant. I will serve them by helping them to remember me. When they remember me, they will also remember where they came from as well. In so doing, they will open a door for my power to enter piercing the veil. Each time my power enters, the veil will weaken a little more, thus not destroying it all at once."

"We still don't understand!" said Michael. "How can you get through the veil since you are made of pure power?"

"Well, Michael, that's the part I haven't mentioned yet. I won't be going in all my glory and power, not by horse, and not with sword. The only way I can enter the garden is to strip myself of all power and enter as one of them."

"No!" shouted Gabriel in desperation. "If you were to go into that place without your power, Jubil would surely destroy you. You know his desire is to kill you!"

"Yes," the King replied. "Wouldn't you die for the ones you love?"

"Yes, your Majesty," said Gabriel, "but there is a big difference between me dying and you. If I died, the kingdom would go on. If you died, all would surely be lost. Jubil would win, and you know what that would mean for the rest of us. He would come here, defeat us, and set himself up as king."

Michael said adamantly, "King Adonai, we cannot let you go there stripped of your power. There must be another way! I will die for you and the Zera. You cannot go; there is too much risk involved."

Then the King said to both of them, "I appreciate your devotion, but this is something only I can do. Jubil will try to kill me; this is true. This is why I must go; remember, the penalty for the Zera's disobedience was death. My plan is to go as one of them and to divert death from them onto me."

"Wait a minute," cried Michael. "They are the guilty ones. Why must you pay?"

"Because they are my children, and because I love them. I will gladly lay down my life for them. The lion will become the sacrificial lamb, but fear not, for this will not be the end!"

"I don't understand! If you lay down your life, how could it not be the end?" Gabriel asked.

"From the beginning, I have prepared for this day. When Jubil attacks, there will still be hope. My power will resurrect me as long as one of the Zera continues to believe!"

"Oh, Lord," said Gabriel, "what if no one believes? Look at how fast they have forgotten you!"

Then the King spoke again, even more sternly than before. "You will have to learn to put more trust in me, Gabriel. I believe in my children, and I know that no matter what happens, they will believe in me! I only wanted you to know because I'm going there tomorrow."

AN UNEXPECTED VISITOR

"What's happening?" asked one of the Malachs as he watched everyone scurrying to the palace.

"The King is leaving today," shouted someone rushing past.

"He's going to the garden to visit the Zera," said another.

As the Malach stood there with his mouth opened wide, another said, "Are you just going to stand there trying to catch flies, or are you going with us to the palace?"

Immediately, he closed his mouth, blushed, and made a beeline to the palace with the rest of them.

At the palace, the King addressed them sharing the details of His trip. Afterwards something happened that boggled their minds—the King sat motionless on His throne while the light of His glory flashed in all directions, then He stood up and stepped forward, leaving the light in its place. The Malachs stared in utter amazement as the King came forth looking exactly like one of His children. It was very odd seeing Him this way, so weak and vulnerable.

The King then said His goodbyes and told all of the Malachs not to worry about Him, for everything would be all right. He then made His way across the kingdom to the sea. He boarded a boat and set sail for the garden. While passing through the edge of the veil in the middle of the sea, He reminisced about how things used to be—remembering how the Zera were when He created them, and then how they changed once they were deceived. He thought about how many of them tried so hard to remember Him, and how many had sailed into the sea searching for the kingdom,

AN UNEXPECTED VISITOR

not realizing that it was hidden from them. He had seen how they searched aimlessly, eventually not even knowing what they were searching for. A tear ran down the King's cheek, dripped, and fell to the deck of the boat. At first, He didn't think anything about it. Then He looked down and noticed the tear drop on the deck near His feet. Suddenly it hit Him—the tear did not cause the ground to tremble. He was just as common as the Zera were now. That sobering thought lingered in the King's mind for a long while.

Jubil now had free reign in the garden. Because of his haughtiness, he believed that victory would soon be his. He laughed as he witnessed the Zera going through life empty, lacking purpose or direction. They reminded him of ants going to and fro, back and forth from their work to their homes without any reason for living, not giving any thought to whether or not their lives could be different. It never even occurred to them that life could be better; they just accepted life as it was.

Many of the Zera were sick or injured, and quite a few were begging in the streets. Some of the Zera had become wealthy, with plenty to eat, while others starved. Some worked hard, and others stole to survive. It was a vicious world, and they had learned to be ruthless and heartless in their quest for survival. The now corrupted Zera had come to believe that integrity and honesty were forms of insanity. Good had become evil, and evil had become good in the eyes of most everyone. Jubil, satisified with the Zera's situation, was very close to activating the final part of his plan. He needed only the few remaining Zera to join him, whereupon, he would have enough reinforcement to attack the kingdom. Unfortunately for Jubil, he had no idea what the King had in store, and thus, was in no way prepared for what lie ahead.

The King arrived at the shoreline of the garden. He hid the boat and made His way to the once serene forest. He couldn't wait to see the Zera face to face. He wasted no time heading in the direction of the waterfall where He had last met with them so long ago. As He walked through the forest, He was burdened by the atrocities surrounding Him. The few trees that remained standing were lifeless, as if rigor mortis had set in. The branches could no longer sway with the wind. They broke, cracked, and fell to the ground. Once lively foliage that covered the forest floor was now brown and brittle and crunched beneath the King's feet. Everything was filthy, covered with soot, and not one animal was there to greet Him. When He arrived at the area that used to be the refreshing waterfall and stood on the banks that once flourished with plush green grass, He sank down to His ankles in mud. The smell was awful. It reeked of death and decay. Dead fish and skeletal remains covered the dirty water and its banks. The dying fish had contaminated the water leaving it unfit for the animals to drink. Beyond the pool, along the stream, many animals lay dead. "This habitation is forsaken and left like a wilderness," stated the King, "for the Zera have forgotten me, they no longer seek me nor have any understanding." The King lamented for the garden. Death truly was His enemy, for what He created to be alive and flourishing was now dried up and lifeless.

The King heard the faint sound of a multitude, like that of many Zera off in the distance, and a bit of joy rose in His heart. He walked in the direction of their voices. As soon as He stepped through the clearing and saw them, He felt overwhelming despair. His joy turned to mourning. There they were, the Zera, who were created in His image, too busy to notice Him, with nothing more on their minds than their own selfish ambitions. The King looked around and saw sick people everywhere. There were blind people, crippled people, and people with sores covering their bodies. Many were begging Him to give them money as He walked by, yet He had no money to give. Others rushed by, pushing the beggars out of their way, yelling at them for obstructing their path. The King was appalled; with a heavy heart, He cried out!

"My dear Zera! What has become of you? You are like sheep that have no shepherd, children that have no parent. You are all moving quickly, but you have no direction. Oh, how often I have longed to gather you together as a hen gathers her chicks under her wings."

AN UNEXPECTED VISITOR

As the King was engulfed with sadness, holding His hands out to them, one of the Zera plowed through the crowd and knocked Him out of the way. The King fell to the ground and experienced pain for the very first time. He sat there stunned. His hands were scratched from falling, and they began to bleed. No one paid any attention to Him; no one bothered to help Him up. As He stood to His feet, He realized that the Zera had hit rock bottom. He knew there was no time to spare. He had come to save them, and He knew by the looks of things, His mission would not be easy.

Without delay, the King walked to the busiest street corner and stood in the middle of the commotion. With everything in Him, He pleaded with the Zera.

"Please, listen to me! I am the King who created you, and I have come here to save you."

The King noticed everyone staring at Him. Then He continued. "Jubil has lied to you and stolen from you leaving you empty with a void inside, but I have come to give you life. Material possessions cannot fill that void, I am what you are seeking; you must believe me!"

"You, sir," the King said to a well dressed Zera. "Listen to me—I have prepared a mansion for you in my kingdom far from here. There is no sickness or trouble there, and whatever you need, you will have. If you will only believe me, I will be able to give you all of it."

"Out of my way," the man grumbled. "I have a very busy schedule, bother someone else."

Then the King turned to a woman passing by and said with much love and compassion, "How about you, my daughter? I want to share my kingdom with you. That is why I created you. If you will believe, you can live with me for eternity."

The woman paused for a moment, giving Him a smug look as if He was strange, and said contentiously, "Live with you? I don't even know you. Can't you see that I am very busy? I have to be at work in five minutes. Now leave me alone."

On and on, the King continued pleading with everyone that walked by. It hurt Him tremendously that not one recognized Him or knew His voice. As He offered His free gift, each one came up with a different excuse for not having time to listen to Him.

One said sarcastically, "I'm sorry, I'm building my house right now; try me next year."

Another laughed and said, "I would love to go with you if I weren't getting married this afternoon."

He heard story after story, excuse after excuse, one more facetious than the next. Even the sick and the poor mocked Him and laughed because of what He was saying.

"Yeah, right," one said. "You're a powerful king, aren't you? If you are so powerful, why do you look so poor? Where are your royal garments? Are they at the cleaners?"

Everyone let out a laugh at the King's expense, but He did not give up hope. The King was determined, believing that someone would remember His voice. There had to be one. Then He noticed a Zera off to His right. This Zera was dressed differently than the rest, and a great many Zera followed him. The King noticed that he was holding *The Book of Remembrance*.

Finally, someone who will surely recognize and remember me, thought the King.

He ran to the Zera and said to him, "I see that you have a copy of *The Book of Remembrance*. Do you know it well?"

"Yes," the Zera replied. "I teach it to all those who long to remember our King."

"Do you remember?" the King asked excitedly.

"Why, yes, I remember. I know our King very well."

"Great," the King said. "Look into my eyes, and tell me what you see. Listen to my voice, and tell me what you hear."

As the Zera looked into His eyes, the King began to speak about many things in the *Book* that described Him in His kingdom and told about His coming.

Then, with a big smile, He said, "Well, what is it that you see? What is it that you hear?"

AN UNEXPECTED VISITOR

The Zera stood there with a blank look on his face, while the King waited to hear what he had to say.

"What I see is a fool, and what I hear is nonsense. You, sir, are definitely no king. You are definitely not this King."

As the Zera and his followers walked away, the King was shocked at the response. To think this Zera was reading the *Book* like He told them to do, and still the darkness was so thick that he couldn't see his King standing right in front of him. The King was growing weary, now realizing how hard it was for the Zera to hear or see Him. He knew before He came that it would be difficult for them, but now He was experiencing it firsthand. He felt empathy for them, for the longer He was there, the more He felt the power of temptation that had destroyed the Zeras' lives. While the Zera scoffed and ridiculed Him, doubt and worry entered His mind. For a moment, He wondered if there was any that would believe. Sometimes the evil around Him was so strong that He Himself began to forget and even questioned who He was. Yet He overcame the temptation. He knew who He was, and He knew that He could not afford to quit now, for the salvation of the Zera was dependent upon the success of His mission.

Days passed with the King standing on the corner crying out, and not one of the Zera would give him the time of day. It was very disheartening for the King; still, He would not stop. He kept calling to them, over and over, pleading with them, asking if anyone would believe and receive His kingdom.

With much conviction and passion He said, "Do you have ears, but fail to hear? Do you have eyes, but fail to see? If one of you would just stop and turn to me, I would heal you."

The Zera just kept scurrying along, supposing another crazy fool had joined their town and wondered when He would be hauled away. But as the King continued to speak, a crippled woman who was begging along the wall of the city was listening to His voice. She had been there watching Him for days, hearing all that He was saying and wished that it could be true.

As He spoke, she said to herself, *Oh, how I would love to believe Him.* She would think about what it would be like to walk again and imagined how wonderful it would be in another kingdom far away without suffering and pain.

Finally, after meditating on it for a while, she thought to herself, *What do I have to lose by believing? Even if He is crazy, I can't be any worse off than I am now.* So she began listening intently to all that He had to say, this time extending her faith.

She opened her heart and believed His words, and began to notice that His voice sounded strangely familiar. It was as if she had heard it before, maybe when she was a child, or maybe in a dream. It was like a voice that she had once known, yet a voice that she could not place. As she listened closer, longing in her heart for what He said to be true, the King looked in her direction. When He did, the woman saw a sparkle flash in His eye. The sparkle was colorful, and it startled her at first. She looked at Him again, and felt like she knew Him as if He was a long, lost relative. The longer she stared at Him, the more she felt drawn to Him.

Suddenly, the feeling compelled her, and without giving any thought to what the others might think of her, she belted out in a loud voice, "I believe You!"

The King stopped in His tracks, turned, and looked directly at her. She was a pitiful sight, lying there with her legs shriveled up, malnourished, and covered with dirt from head to toe.

As the King walked toward her, she said it again, "I believe You!"

At this the others began yelling at her telling her to be quiet.

Ignoring them, the King looked directly into her eyes. When He did, He saw who she was, and He wept bitterly—partly from sorrow, and partly from joy.

"Karen," He said, "I have found you."

The woman looked up at Him in utter amazement. "How did you know my name?" Tears welled up in her eyes. "I haven't heard my name spoken in so long, and it's nice to hear someone say it."

AN UNEXPECTED VISITOR

Then the King said to her, "Karen, I am King Adonai, don't you remember me?"

Karen looked at Him again, and then she saw something that left her astonished. For a moment, while looking into His eyes, she saw Him in all His glory. It was at that moment she knew that He truly was the King. She fell prostrate at His feet, her arm covering her face in shame as she thought about her past. She remembered being with Him in His throne room and how she used to dance by the seashore, vowing that she would never forget Him. She couldn't believe that she had forgotten her King and wondered how she could have been so deceived and so blind. As she wept, she noticed that she was soaking His feet with her tears, so she began drying them with her hair. The Zera walking near by wondered what she was doing. They pointed their fingers at her and laughed. The King reached down and touched her on the shoulder, saying, "Karen, your faith has saved you."

When the King touched her shoulder, His power was drawn from the throne, through Him, and into her. At once, color shot forth from her body. First her eyes sparkled and changed to a bright blue, then her hair turned to a golden blonde; her skin turned from gray to a rich tan color, and her clothes became bright and colorful. Not a soul on the street was moving. Nobody was mocking anymore. Everyone gathered around to see this miraculous sight. No one could even remember what color looked like any more. It was now that they realized the King, too, had color, but they were too blind to notice. Karen saw her colorful clothes and skin; she jumped to her feet and began to shout. She was so happy that she didn't even realize that her legs were healed. She was as light as a feather, dancing and shouting and thanking the King.

Tears streamed down the King's face as she danced. He knew that someone would believe, and who better than His lovely Karen. After witnessing what the King had done for her, other Zera began to believe as well. When they did, they saw Him in His glory and remembered Him just as Karen had.

REMEMBER

They ran to Him, fell before Him and vehemently cried out, "I believe you! I believe you are King Adonai!"

When the King touched them, color began to appear on all of them, and He restored each of them to their original state. He loved them so much and hated watching them suffer. As more of the Zera were redeemed, the news about the King began to spread across the land. Many more came to Him, believed the good news about the kingdom, and were healed as well.

As Karen watched the miracles that were taking place, her past once again flashed before her eyes. She began to remember Gary and her children, Luke and Jake. It had been so long since she had seen them that she had virtually forgotten them, but now she remembered that they had somehow drifted apart when Gary started serving Jubil.

Karen went to the King and said to Him anxiously, "King Adonai, you must help my family; I have not seen them for years. You must help me find them."

The King said, "Karen, my daughter, trust in me and everything will be all right. You and your family will be reunited!"

"Yes, I believe we will," said Karen, now filled with a newfound joy. She knew that someday she would be with her family, and that together they would be with their true father in His kingdom for all eternity.

LOVE TRIUMPHS

"Jubil, Jubil, something strange is happening in the garden," said Gary, exhausted from running to the prison. Jubil was basking in his presumed victory as Gary entered.

"In the garden?" asked Jubil.

"Yes," said Gary. "A stranger is there helping the Zera."

"Helping them? Why does that concern me?" said Jubil, leaning back in his chair, adoring himself in a mirror, while one of the Rah Malachs fed him grapes and another massaged his shoulders.

"Well, when he touches them, they instantly change."

"Change?" said Jubil, now edging up on his seat.

"Yes, when he touches them, they suddenly become colorful. The lame are walking, the blind can see, and the deaf can hear."

"Are you saying that the Zera are being healed?" responded Jubil, now in frustration.

"Yes," said Gary.

"Did this stranger say who He was?"

"Yes, everyone is calling Him King Adonai," replied Gary.

"King Adonai? King Adonai is here!?" Jubil was wringing his hands together.

"Should I know him?" asked Gary.

"No! He must be an imposter. I will take care of this, Gary, you can go now."

Gary left wondering who this King Adonai might be, while Jubil told the Rah Malachs who were present to go and gather the others for an emergency meeting.

REMEMBER

One hour later the Rah Malachs assembled before Jubil. Jubil, hostile, screamed, "How did He get here? How did He get through the veil?"

The Rah Malachs were confused and wondered what he was talking about.

Jubil, aware of their confusion, began to explain. "Somehow the King has entered the garden, and He is healing the Zera and restoring their memories."

"How?" asked one of the Rah Malachs.

"I don't know," shouted Jubil. "That's what I'm trying to figure out."

Then one of the Rah Malachs, who went to gather the others, spoke up and said, "I think I have seen the King."

"Go on," snipped Jubil.

The Rah Malach continued, "I saw a stranger standing in the town square. I didn't recognize Him, although now that you mention it, it must have been the King."

"Ok, that's apparent, but how did he get here?" asked Jubil, almost in a panic.

"I don't know," said the Rah Malach. "If he is the King, he sure looked different."

"What do you mean, different?" snarled Jubil.

"Well, he didn't have any light. In fact, He looked like one of the Zera."

"He didn't have His light?" said Jubil, sounding hopeful.

"No," answered the Rah Malach.

"Hmmmm." Jubil thought for a moment, and then said, "If He doesn't have His light, then maybe He doesn't have His power. That must be how He entered the garden. He came without His power! What a fool!" exclaimed Jubil, now pacing back and forth with excitement.

"If He doesn't have His power with Him, how is He healing the Zera?" asked another Rah Malach.

The Rah Malachs looked at each other, shrugging their shoulders and shaking their heads.

Then the one that saw the King spoke up. "It must be that light that comes from the sky and enters their bodies. After that happens, it seems like they are empowered."

"What do you mean *empowered*?" asked Jubil.

"It's like Gary said. They get their color back, and then they are healed. Many are coming to the King now, and all of them are leaving with His power in them," said the Rah Malach.

"Then we must stop Him," snapped Jubil. "We must stop Him from doing any more damage than He already has."

Jubil thought long and hard, then, after several minutes, he boldly held up the key that was around his neck and shouted in an angry voice, "I've got it! By the power of this key, I speak death to the King!"

A Rah Malach spoke up and asked, "Can you do that? Can you kill the King?"

Jubil sneered, "Oh, yes, I can. He has no power here. He's in my kingdom now, and I hold the power of life and death."

Again, Jubil spoke curses over the King, and then told the Rah Malachs to make sure the Zera did not believe the King. The Rah Malachs left at once and did as Jubil said. They found the Zera that taught from *The Book of Remembrance* and told him that the stranger was an imposter, just as he had suspected. They warned the Zera that this stranger would deceive many and steal all of his followers if he didn't stop him.

Immediately, the Zera with the *Book* began speaking out against the stranger, and many of the Zera listened. Most of them esteemed him and respected his opinion.

As crowds gathered around the Zera with the *Book*, he said, "Look at these so-called believers. This stranger is performing magic tricks, just an imitation of what the true King can do. If this stranger was the true King, He would have saved us all and taken us out of this place. Look at Him! He doesn't have a great light like the King in the Book, without His light He has no real power. Many began to listen to the Zera with the *Book*, and many of them became indignant toward the King. Contention filled the streets as some chose to believe the King and be healed, while others grumbled against Him, wanting Him to go away. The more the King healed people, the angrier the others became.

"We have to stop this nonsense," shouted a Zera, filled with hostility.

(No one knew that it was Jubil in disguise.)

"This stranger is deceiving us and giving us false hope with His lies. If we care about our family at all, we have to do something."

"Like what?" someone asked.

"We should kill Him!" said that Zera quite forcefully.

"Kill Him?" they gasped. They were angry, but killing Him seemed a little drastic.

"Yes," he replied. "Don't you see that the only way to keep the others from believing this traitor is to kill Him right in front of them? Surely, if He is the true King, no one will be able to kill Him. If they see Him die, they will know that He is a phony."

The crowd was speechless, until finally the Zera with the *Book* spoke up. "He's right; we must serve the true King who was written about in this book, and kill the imposter."

The crowds' conscience was eased after hearing the Zera with the *Book* agree. With him involved, it somehow seemed like the right thing to do now.

Finally, everyone began cheering and shouting, "Kill Him! Kill Him!"

Suddenly, the crowd became a frenzied mob, growing more and more violent.

As they gathered around the King, His followers pleaded with them, saying, "What are you doing? Can't you see that this is the King?" The more they tried to deter them, the more determined the mob became.

The believers turned to the King. "Do something! Tell them who you are."

The King kept quiet, like a lamb being led to the slaughter. Finally, the mob grabbed hold of the King and brought Him before the Zera with the *Book* to be questioned. Still, the King would not say a word. They laughed at Him and mocked Him, yet the King held His tongue. While the King was being questioned, they blindfolded Him, spit on Him, and slapped His face. A Zera jeered the King and said, "If you are the King, tell me who just slapped you?" Everyone laughed. They did everything they could to get Him to react, and yet He did nothing in His defense.

As the believers watched the King being tortured, they wondered why the true King would take that abuse without doing something about it. The Zera with the *Book* released the King to the crowd, saying, "Do you have something to say for yourself? Please tell me. Are you King Adonai?"

"It is as you say," said the King.

"You heard Him," shouted the Zera with the Book, "do with Him what you will."

The crowd grew more aggressive.

Jubil, still disguised, yelled, "Kill Him now!"

With Jubil provoking them, the crowd ran toward the King, snarling and growling. They were acting like mindless animals, like puppets hanging by Jubil's strings. At once, they began hitting, punching, slapping, and scratching the King. They pulled His hair out and tore His clothes, but the King did not resist. Those who believed gathered around, trying to stop them. Some of the believers ran off crying, feeling sorrow for the King. Others left feeling very disappointed in Him for not defending Himself. As the beating continued, the King fell to the ground, and in a fit of madness, like sharks in a feeding frenzy, all of them began kicking Him viciously.

Many of the believers were afraid for their own lives and fled. Many stopped believing in Him, and turned back to their old gray selves, and joined in cursing the King.

After a few moments, the Zera grew tired of torturing the King. Motionless, He lay there, blood covered His body and every eye was on Him. Two Zera grabbed Him and stood Him up next to a tree. He stood there weak and helpless, just like any other Zera would look. The color drained from His body. His eyes were blackened, His face bruised, and His mouth bloodied. His clothes were nearly torn completely off. Bruises were forming on His body where they had kicked Him, and clods of hair were hanging out from His head. He could not stand on His own strength, so the two Zera held Him up, taunting Him.

"Is this our King?" they asked. "If He is our King, why can't He save Himself? If He can't save Himself, how can He ever save us?"

Everyone laughed and shouted crude comments. Suddenly, Karen came running up, forcing her way through the crowd.

She fell down before Him, then looked up at the crowd, and in a loud voice said, "Stop it! Stop it! He is our King. Can't you see that He has come to help us and to heal us? Look at me! All of you know me. You know that I was crippled, and now I can walk. He is the true King! He only wanted to help us! He didn't come to harm us. Why can't any of you see how much He loves us? Look at Him. Can you not see that He is willing to lay down His life for us?" Karen looked for sympathy, but she found none!

The King looked at Karen proudly, trying to smile. He was beaten so badly she could hardly recognize him. Her eyes brimmed with tears. Then like a flood, the tears gushed forth from her eyes as she wept. Karen's words and selfless actions finally pierced the heart of the crowd. How pitiful and helpless the King looked. Suddenly, their hearts broke with compassion, and they started feeling bad about what they were doing.

As everyone began to back off and let the King go, Jubil suddenly burst through the crowd, bearing a sword in his hand. Before anyone could think, Jubil walked up to the King and stabbed him through the heart. Jubil tried desperately to keep his disguise as one of the Zera, but his anger caused him to transform into his true nature, a hideous beast, and then in a flash back to himself. Everyone was shocked as they looked at Jubil and then back at the King. Jubil had jammed the sword in so hard that it pinned the King to the tree.

Jubil's eyes were blood red as he turned to the crowd. "Now you can see that this imposter is no king at all."

LOVE TRIUMPHS

The King's head hung down and blood began to drip from his mouth. The two Zera holding him let go, and the King slumped over, hanging from the tree.

Instantly, like a mother losing her only son, Karen jumped up crying, "No, no, you can't die! You're my only hope, please don't die."

The King raised His head one last time and tried to reach His hand out to Karen in an effort to somehow comfort her. In His eyes, Karen saw a sparkle of hope and an undying love, assuring her that everything would be all right.

Karen smiled for a moment, thinking the King could not die so easily, then her smile quickly faded.

The spark dimmed and the King's eyes grew heavy. Then He spoke His last dying words, "It is finished." He let out a long wheezing exhale and collapsed on the sword, hanging from the tree.

"No!" shrieked Karen. "It can't be!"

Jubil let out a gratifying laugh as he watched the King die. *I can't believe it was this easy,* thought Jubil. *I have dreamed of this moment, knowing that some day I would have the pleasure of watching the King take His last breath! Soon I will be seated on the throne, and I will receive the worship I deserve.*

Everyone gawked in horror, while Karen cried bitter tears.

Then Jubil turned to the crowd and shouted, "Look at Him now! Does this man look like a powerful King to you? Could the King who created all of you die this easily?"

Before Jubil could finish his last word, the garden began to shake violently. The tree from which the King was hanging split down the middle and everyone fell to the ground trembling.

At that very moment, the Malachs back in the kingdom also fell down and called out, "King Adonai, King Adonai, what is happening?"

Jubil stood up, brushed himself off, and tried to sound confident. "He was right, it is finished! Now I'm the king!"

Karen looked up at him, and with disgust in her voice, said, "You are no king!"

Jubil wanted to slap her, but he feared that she still had the King's power on the inside of her. Karen got up and walked through the crowd as everyone stared.

Jubil cleared his throat, trying to regain his composure. "It's over now. Everyone can go." Jubil then turned to two of the Rah Malachs that were with him and said, "Pick Him up; take Him to the prison."

The Rah Malachs spirits lifted, relieved that they had eluded the King's judgment, they cheerfully picked up the King and dragged Him away. When they arrived at the prison, all the Rah Malachs were gloating over Jubil's glorious victory. They watched as the two carried the King past the massive gates, down to the darkest, gloomiest cell in the bottom of the prison where Jubil had been chained. They tossed the King in and locked the door, binding it with very strong chains.

Even though the King was dead, Jubil still had one more task to accomplish. He needed to thwart the testimonies of those that had been healed, so he called Gary to take his place as right-hand man and thanked him for revealing the alleged imposter. He then put the twins, Luke and Jake, in charge of organizing a group to stop, what Jubil called, *this madness.*

So immediately, Luke and Jake set out on their mission to convince the Zera that Jubil was the only true king. It was easy to do now that King Adonai was dead. Color began disappearing from the land once again as the Zera succumbed to their doubts and fears.

Michael and Gabriel watched the flame in the throne room diminish more and more as each new believer turned away.

"What the King came here to do was only in vain," said Jubil.

Then one of the Rah Malachs said, "Yes, this was easy. The King's plan seems to have backfired. I think almost everyone has turned back to serving you, I mean, that is, except…"

Before he could get the name out of his mouth, Jubil snapped back. "Except whom?"

The Rah Malach said apprehensively, "Well, we haven't located Karen quite yet."

"Karen?" shouted Jubil. "Where is she?"

"We have no idea," the Rah Malach said defensively.

"That's not good enough, we must find her now! We can't afford for Karen to believe in the King any longer. She is too dangerous!"

Jubil and the Rah Malachs set out searching for Karen. They looked through every village, searching high and low throughout the garden. She was not in the forest or near the stream nor was she down by the sea. Jubil was furious.

"There can only be one place left," he said. "She must have snuck down to the prison, blast her!"

Jubil and the Rah Malachs ran toward the prison and searched there; still, she was nowhere to be found. They searched outside the prison throughout the valley, but still, to no avail. As they walked back to the prison, Jubil thought he heard something. Suddenly it dawned on him, he remembered the crevice that Aaron and Eden had hidden in when they came to speak to him when he was locked up in the prison. Jubil went over to the crevice in the wall. He could hear Karen crying. She was not trying to hide. She only wanted to be near her King. Jubil listened as she talked to the King whom she hoped was there.

"Why did you have to die? I so wanted to believe in you. I believed you were the King. How could you forsake me? How could you leave me alone?"

As Jubil peeked around the corner, he noticed that she had a few gray spots on her body, just like the others. Listening to what Karen was saying made Jubil realize that she was losing all hope in the King.

Jubil calmly stepped out and said with a soft voice, "Hello, Karen."

Karen was surprised. She hesitantly looked up at Jubil.

"I see that you wanted to believe He was the King," Jubil said as gently as possible.

Karen did not answer.

"I know how much you want to believe in this fairy tale about the King and the so-called imaginary kingdom. It's just not true, my dear," said Jubil. "This is your life, Karen, this is all it will ever be."

"What about my color and my legs? They're healed!" said Karen.

"I don't believe it!" Jubil replied. "Look, your color is already beginning to fade and your legs, how are they feeling right now?"

Karen looked down and noticed the gray spots on her arm. As soon as she saw the spots, she felt her legs becoming weak. She looked up at Jubil with tears in her eyes, and Jubil looked back at her with the most concerned and loving look that he could conjure.

Michael and Gabriel watched as the light flickered above the throne, looking as if it was about to go out.

Karen looked back down at her legs that were growing weaker by the second and said forlornly, "I guess you're right, Jubil."

As she spoke, the light in the throne room flickered one last time, and then extinguished. The smoke that had been rising in the throne room settled down to the floor, then the floor's bright luster turned dull and gray. The palace began to shake and small pebbles and dust began falling from the ceiling. It became dark and gloomy throughout the Kingdom. The Malachs shook uncontrollably. They had never experienced darkness before, and had no idea what was happening.

Meanwhile, at the prison, Jubil pretended to comfort Karen as she wept. He tried to hold back the laughter while saying to her, "Everything will be all right, Karen. I am your king now."

When Karen heard what he said, she looked at him with disgust. "This can't be." She announced, feeling like a fool for even talking with him for a moment. As she turned to rebuke him sharply, she noticed the key around his neck. The moment she looked at it, it sparkled and then turned dull and gray. It reminded her of the sparkle that she saw in the King's eyes that day when He was dying. Instantly it hit her like a ton of bricks.

"That's it!" shouted Karen. "Love is the key! The King believed in us even when we did not believe in Him. He died for us even though we were His enemy. That's what it's all about, believing even when everything is stacked against you. That is what the King was showing me with his eyes."

Instantly, Karen was released from Jubil's spell. The spark that had extinguished in the throne room suddenly ignited inside of her. The power had never died. It had only been hidden in her heart.

She jumped to her feet and shouted at the top of her lungs, "I believe, I believe, I believe you, my King!"

Jubil jumped back, startled, nearly falling to the ground. The key on his neck glistened and then shined bright again. Simultaneously at the palace, the shaking ceased, and the light in the throne room began to flicker, and smoke began to rise from the floor. Michael and Gabriel looked at each other with a shimmer of hope, then the light burst forth, burning brighter than ever. Gabriel and Michael shouted loudly, filling the palace with cheer and jubilation. Basil joined in, along with all the Malachs, and rejoicing filled the throne room.

Light descended like a falling star from the throne room and burst into the prison cell.

Jubil ran inside the prison and hollered to the Rah Malachs, "Open His cell! Quick, open His cell!"

A Rah Malach unlocked the cell where the King had been laid, and as he opened the door, a great light shone into his eyes. Horrified, he hid his face. Jubil was too angry to be afraid. He flung the door open, and to his dismay, his greatest nightmare stood before him. It was the King, alive and well, in all His glory.

Jubil looked at the King in shock and said, "You're alive? You were dead! I killed you myself."

The King said, "Love has lifted me, I am the living one; I was dead, and now look, I am alive forever and ever! You never did understand my greatest gift, did you Jubil?"

"Gift? What gift?"

"The gift of love," said the King. "Can you not see it yet? The greatest power was never in your strength or your beauty. It was never in your music or in your great ability to run or fly. The greatest gift that I had given you was love, and you failed to see that. You failed to see the power of love; I loved the Zera and believed in them. I believed that at least one of them would, in return, believe in me. Because I loved them, I put my trust in them. When I came here, I knew you would try to kill me. I also knew that my power could not die as long as one of my Zera continued to believe in me. Karen believed me because she loved me. Love is the power that raised me from the dead, and as you can see, love has triumphed over death!"

Then Jubil said angrily, "Well, there is one thing you overlooked. I have not forgotten what you told the Zera on the hill that day. You said that if they believed me, they would surely die and end up with the same fate. As you see, all of them have failed you. You may have been brought back to life, but I will make sure that all of them die, including your lovely Karen."

The King smiled and Jubil felt uneasy. "That is where you are wrong, Jubil. You still don't see what happened, do you? When I came here, I only came for one reason, to die!"

Jubil's eyes grew wider.

"You were right to say that the punishment for the Zera was death. It was only in death that I could show the greatness of my love for them. Don't you see? As one of them, I could enter through the veil, take their punishment, and die in their place, the just for the unjust. Because I died, they don't have to, and because I rose from the dead, they too will be able to rise to live with me forever in my kingdom."

At that, the King reached out and snatched the key from around Jubil's neck. "I'll be taking this!"

Jubil trembled like a scolded, helpless child.

The King walked toward the prison gate, and as He approached it, it flung wide open. He walked out with all of His power and glory. Jubil stood there, his mouth hanging open, with a look of utter confusion and failure. When he realized that killing the King helped the children, he knew that the King had made a spectacle of him in front of everyone.

He cried out in frustration, "Nooooo!"

As the King stepped out of the prison, He noticed Karen standing at the foot of the hill. "Karen!" He said, smiling from ear to ear.

When Karen saw the King alive, her spots instantly vanished restoring her color, and her legs regained their strength. She jumped to her feet, shouted, and ran to the King. "I knew you were the King! I knew it was true!" Falling at His feet, she held onto them.

The King was elated. He said, "I knew it would be you that believed, my daughter. We don't have much time. Go to the other Zera and tell them 'the King is alive!'"

A SAFE RETURN

Karen ran as quickly as she could, searching for anyone who would listen to her. She knew there had to be someone who would believe her. The first place she went was a friend's house where many believers used to gather. She barged in through the door shouting, "He's alive! He's alive!"

"Who is alive?" they asked curiously.

"The King is alive! He has risen!" said Karen with new hope.

"Did you say the King is alive?"

"We watched Him die with our own eyes!" one exclaimed.

Still another said, "I would like to believe He's alive, but I would have to see Him and touch Him to believe it."

Even as he was speaking, the King stepped through the door.

"You were saying," said the King.

Everyone abruptly looked at the King with surprise. Their questions were satisfied, and they believed.

Upon believing, their color was restored, and each was made whole. The King was pleased to see these few Zera colorful and happy, like He created them to be, but His gift was not just for them. These would be His witnesses to testify of His resurrection. For the King so loved all the Zera, that He gave His life, so that through Him, all of them could be saved. He wanted every Zera to come to the knowledge of the truth, for it was truth that would set them free.

"Go into all the garden and spread the good news of the kingdom. Those who believe will be healed. Tell them that I have delivered them from the power of darkness, and if they endure, I will convey them into my kingdom," said the King. "I want everyone to hear this message—that I am alive. Be strong and take courage, know that I have overcome Jubil, and I have taken back the key to life and death. Jubil has no power over you now. Remember, there is power in unity, so let nothing divide you, and whatever you do resist the evil one. Draw close to me, and I will draw close to you. Resist him, and he will flee. Remember who you are, you are overcomers, heirs to my throne, great and mighty warriors."

As the King finished speaking, He vanished as quickly as He had arrived.

Instantly, the King appeared back in the kingdom. All the Malachs were waiting there for Him, and shouted with exuberant joy as they welcomed Him home.

Gabriel, thrilled at the sight of the King, spoke first, "I'm so happy to see you, your Majesty. I am sorry I ever doubted you."

Then Michael, enthused, said, "I never doubted for a moment."

Gabriel looked at Michael with surprise, and then Michael's face lit up, "All right, I guess I was worried a little bit. Welcome back, Your highness."

At that, everyone laughed, including the King.

Then Basil chimed in. "I too was worried, my Lord. What purpose would there be for worship if you were not here? Welcome home, my King."

The Malachs surrounded the King, picked Him up on their shoulders, and made their way back to the palace. They set their great King down at the door, waiting for Him to lead them into the palace.

As they entered the throne room, the King paused for a moment to reflect on what had just taken place. "Okay," He said. "I guess I must tell you that I too had my doubts while I was there. It is good indeed to be home."

The King sat on His throne in the midst of the light and was restored to His original state. Everyone, at once, in perfect unity, bowed before the King. His power surged through each of them, and they were filled with unexplainable joy. Basil grabbed his harp, and along with the other musicians, began to play, celebrating late into the night.

The next day, when Basil, Michael, and Gabriel came to the throne room, the King told them about His plans, forthwith.

"Gabriel, you and your messengers are to continue speaking my word of knowledge like you have been, although this time with more urgency. Tell all of the messengers to find a part of the veil that has already become weakened and speak to the Zeras' hearts as loudly as they can in hopes that they will hear them. Compel the Zera to search for me and to find me. When the final one hears and believes, the veil will be vulnerable. When that glorious moment comes, we will return for my children."

"Yes, Lord, we will do as you say," said Gabriel.

Then the King turned to Michael and said, "Prepare the warriors; there is little time left. Soon we will be going to retrieve the Zera, just as I told you."

"Yes, King Adonai, we will be prepared."

Throughout the garden, those who had witnessed the resurrection burst into action, reaching out to as many of the Zera as possible. As they pressed forward, it seemed as if they were covered with a cloak of indescribable grace. Even with Jubil and his Rah Malachs' lurking presence, they weren't afraid. They were eager to share the awesome good news with everyone.

It was amazing what happened when they started telling the story about the King returning to life. Each time they shared the news, many believed and were changed. It was as if the King was there Himself, multiplied by many. When they believed, light blasted into them and color suddenly appeared all over their bodies. If they were sick or crippled, they were instantly healed. It wasn't long before the number that believed increased dramatically. Happiness was filling the garden once again; light and color appeared in small parts of the land, grass sprouted, flowers blossomed, trees budded, and a section of the stream became clear.

Many of the past leaders heard and believed again, like Ryan and Jared, the sons of Aaron. Karen and the others welcomed all the new believers and encouraged them to share the good news about the King and His return. Many gathered together and reminisced about old times. Karen and some other leaders taught new believers about what happened while the King was with them, and then added it to *The Book of Remembrance*. They wanted everyone throughout time to be able to read what had occurred. Better yet, they especially wanted everyone to know the King was coming back again very soon.

Jubil, on the other hand, sat in darkness inside the prison, appearing gloomy and depressed.

"Why me? How did I get in this mess?" he squalled. His words revealed that self pity was consuming him. "I loathe the King and the Zera. I curse the day they were born."

Day after day Jubil sat there, moaning and groaning, worrying because he knew his time was running out. He knew that the King was going to return for the Zera. He knew that would be the great and terrible day, great for the Zera, terrible for him. The Rah Malachs were acting even worse than Jubil. They were all lying around like a bunch of infants, whining and complaining, curled up in the fetal position.

"Why did we listen to you, Jubil? Now look at us; what will happen to us when the King returns?" they all grumbled.

"Quiet!" shouted Jubil. "Can't you see that I am thinking here? What are all of you doing just lying there like lumps on a log? Does anybody know what is going on up in the garden? Has anyone been watching the Zera?"

"Why, no, Jubil, we've been right here with you," said one of the Rah Malachs squirming on the floor.

"Then get up!" shouted Jubil. "Get up and go look in the garden to see what the Zera are doing."

At once, they jumped to their feet and headed toward the garden, leaving Jubil alone to wallow in self-pity. After spying on the Zera, the Rah Malachs returned to the prison and reported what they saw.

REMEMBER

"It's worse than we thought," said a Rah Malach. "Many of the Zera believe again! In fact, color is not only appearing on them, it is coming back to parts of the garden as well. They seem to be driving the darkness out of the land somehow. How is this possible?"

"It's His power, you fool," said Jubil angrily. "Don't you get it? Each time one of them believes, they receive the King's power. Not only are we going to suffer in this place for eternity, but we won't even get the pleasure of watching any of them suffer with us. The King told me that if they believe in Him, even though they had turned away, His death would pay the price so they could live in His kingdom forever. It's just not fair."

The Rah Malachs sat with bloodshot eyes, their chins resting on their hands. They looked as if they wanted to quit.

One of them said, "You're right, it's not fair; all they have to do is believe and they're saved!"

"What if they don't believe?" asked another.

"What did you say?" asked Jubil.

Nervously, he responded, "I said, uh, what happens to them if they don't believe?"

"That's it!" shouted Jubil. The Rah Malach ducked in fear for his life, thinking Jubil would lash out at him.

Jubil proceeded to speak, prancing around like a rooster. "The battle's not over yet, nothing has changed at all." His eyes lit up.

"Yes, He did die for them, but if they choose not to believe it, it won't help them. Listen up, we are in a war, and if we are going to win, we cannot give up so easily. Maybe the King has turned up the heat a little bit and swayed the odds against us, but that doesn't mean we can't turn up the heat as well. What are we doing sitting here? The King may have won one battle, but we can still win this war."

As the Rah Malach's gathered to listen closely, Jubil explained. "We have to speak into their hearts this time and reach deep into their souls, telling them any lie we can think of."

"Like what?" asked one of the Rah Malachs.

"I don't care what you say. Tell them there are many kings to choose from, or just tell them there is no King," said Jubil.

A Rah Malach spoke up and asked, "How can we tell them there is no King? How can we possibly convince them that they have no creator? What will we tell them when they ask us where they came from?"

"Again, I don't care what you tell them!" shouted Jubil. "For all I care, you can tell them they evolved from monkeys."

"What! Surely they wouldn't believe something as outrageous as that," said a Rah Malach.

"Just do it!" shouted Jubil. "I also want you to gather up sickness, disease, and death, and take it to all the Zera you find."

"How can we do that? We don't have the power of the key anymore," said a Rah Malach.

"Silence!" screamed Jubil. "Just listen to what I tell you. We may not have the power of the key, but the Zera do. For their tongue has the power of life and death; I will turn their own tongues against them! All we have to do is control what they say. Go to them and whisper in their ears every negative, discouraging, faithless word that you can think of. I want them speaking sickness and death over themselves. Every time they feel the slightest pain or ailment, I want them speaking it into existence. Each time they speak something negative over themselves, every kind of cancer, flu, heart attack, stroke, liver disease, and every other kind of sickness will come upon them. They will become crippled, blind, deaf, and dumb. If they come up with a cure for one disease, then another will appear, worse than the one before. I may not hold the power of death anymore, but I do retain the power of words."

Jubil gathered yet another group and began giving them their orders. "I want to see fighting and wars amongst the Zera. I want the Zera divided. I want their hatred for each other to be stronger than ever, and I want them to be filled with every kind of prejudice."

"How, master?" asked a Rah Malach.

Jubil turned to him and said with the most sinister voice, "Tell some that they are greater than others. Teach them to make slaves of each other. Soon hatred will run deep through generations to come. There will be no hope for the fury that will rage within them. The seed that will be planted will give birth to the greatest of all evils, hatred of their fellow brothers."

Jubil then turned to another Rah Malach and said, "I want you to contact Gary and tell him to meet me here tomorrow. Then I want a few of you to raise up new leaders among the Zera and cause them to turn against any remaining believers. I want every true believer stamped out any way you can. This will be our greatest victory ever. We will speak death and destruction into every one of the Zera, and, then, just as I planned before, I will let them do the killing for me. One last thing, gather the leaders like Jared, Ryan, Luke, and Jake, and coerce them to join us. If they refuse, kill them! I assure you, when I am finished, there will be many more of the Zera on our side than believers in the King. The King will be very surprised when He comes to collect the Zera. He will be sorry He ever left. I can't wait to see His face. In the end, if there are any believers that manage to stay alive, they will feel my wrath on that day."

At once, the Rah Malachs set out to do Jubil's bidding.

JUBIL'S REVENGE

The next day Gary met with Jubil, unaware of what had taken place in the garden. Gary and his two sons had been so hoodwinked by Jubil's witchery that news of the King's victory and resurrection eluded them completely. For all they knew the imposter who claimed to be the King was dead, and everything would be getting back to normal.

"You called for me?" said Gary.

"Why, yes," said Jubil. "I called for you because you are my most loyal and trusted friend. I have a special mission for you, and I believe you will be perfect for this job."

"What is it?" inquired Gary.

"I want you to locate Karen. You do remember Karen, don't you?"

"Of course, how could I forget? From what I hear, she is crazier now than when she first refused to join us."

"She is crazy all right," spouted Jubil. "Not only is she out of her mind, but she is influencing the other Zera as well."

"So I've heard," said Gary.

Then Jubil looked deep into Gary's eyes and said, "If you care anything about your fellow Zera, and if you care anything about me, you will stop her."

"Stop her? How can I do that? What, do you want me to arrest her for being crazy?"

"No!" spewed Jubil. "I want you to kill her!"

Gary, dumbfounded, took a deep breath. "Kill her? You want me to kill Karen?"

"You heard me correctly," said Jubil, "Not only do I want you to kill her, I want you to kill all those who believe like her."

Gary, felt sick to his stomach. He knew that he had sworn his allegiance to Jubil, but this was asking way too much.

"Why must we kill them? I know that they are a thorn in our flesh, and they interfere with our mission, but kill them?"

Jubil, noticing that this was hard for Gary to accept, said very convincingly, "Don't you see what is happening here, Gary? Karen has been infected in the worst way. This is not harmless propaganda she is spreading; she is telling everyone that the Zera I killed is the King. She says that He rose from the dead and that He's coming back to rescue the Zera from this place. What's worse is she really believes it. Surely, you can see that she is turning the Zera against me? We almost had unity. We were a family, and now she is causing dissension. Is that what you want, Gary? Do you really want our family to fall apart? Look at the increase of fighting and bickering among the Zera. Look at the influx of sickness and disease. Karen and the believers look like they are getting healed, and in return, it seems as if everyone else is getting sick and dying. Can we just sit back and let this happen, or are we going to do the right thing and stop it before it destroys us all?"

Gary pondered what Jubil was saying, and then with a sigh, answered, "I guess you are right. I never really thought of it that way. I see now that we don't have a choice. I will do as you say."

"Good," said Jubil, concealing a wicked smile.

As soon as Gary was gone, Jubil made his way down into the bowels of the prison where the Rah Malachs were holding Jared and Ryan prisoners. They refused to serve Jubil and continued to pledge their allegiance to the King. Jubil walked down the long, dark steps that curved along the edge of the wall, descending into the lowest part of the prison and entered the room where they were being held. Ryan and Jared were yelling at the Rah Malachs, demanding their release, while the Rah Malachs held spears to their throats.

Jubil shouted to Ryan and Jared, "Quiet!" and then told the Rah Malachs, "I will deal with these two." Slowly, he walked over to Ryan, snarling and glaring in intimidation, hoping he would succumb to his wishes.

Ryan looked directly at Jubil and said, very boldly, "I will never serve you!" Then he spit on Jubil.

Jubil, livid, wiped the spit off his face while transforming into a hideous beast. His face was now grotesque with large fangs and sunken eyes. His head stretched into the shape of a dragon, while his wings and body turned to dark leather with scales. Slowly, his back popped and twisted—huge spikes erupted at each vertebra; his eyes flared, and smoke filtered through his large nostrils. Jubil held up his razor-clawed hands and grabbed Ryan by the throat, pushing him against the wall.

"You don't have a choice in the matter, now do you? You will serve me or you will die!"

Right then Jared shouted, "We would rather die than serve you!"

"That will be my pleasure," growled Jubil. He turned, extended his sharp claw, and stabbed Ryan in the heart. Ryan gasped and clutched his chest. Blood ran through his fingers; his vision grew dim as his arms fell to his side. Jubil let him fall to the stony ground. Life left him and his eyes turned cloudy.

"Nooo!" cried Jared.

Jubil grabbed his sword. "Would you still rather die than serve me?"

You could see the anger in Jared's eyes. Death did not frighten him in the least. Jared leaped to his feet and charged Jubil, knocking the sword from his hand. He jumped on Jubil and tried to choke him, but Jubil was just too big and strong. Jubil laughed and threw Jared to the ground. He shook the sweat from his brow, picked up the sword, and walked slowly toward Jared, who looked up through a haze of semi-consciousness. Jared tried to get up, but could only turn his head, barely keeping his eyes open. He watched, defenseless, as Jubil swung his sword, severing his hand that was extended forward to block the strike.

Jared's eyes widened from the unimaginable pain. The blood from his hand revealed the reality of the wound, and the shock of it caused him to try frantically to escape, but before Jared could stand, Jubil thrust the sword into his neck, piercing his main artery. Jared fell to the floor. At first, each time his heart beat, blood pulsated from the wound; now it merely ebbed. Cold shivers came over his body. He looked at his brother lying on the floor next to him and remembered the King's words of victory, all the while wondering how this could be happening. Jared's strength faded, life flowed from his body, and his eyes glossed at the sound of Jubil's laughs.

Outside in the garden, Gary gathered nonbelievers to help him fight against the so-called traitors. His boys, Luke and Jake, were the first to be recruited. They had seen what believing had done to their mother, how it healed her, but at the same time seemed to make her insane. They were eager to join their father, but then Gary told the boys about Jubil's plan to eliminate all believers, including their mother.

"There has to be another way!" declared the twins. "We can't kill our own mother."

They tried reasoning with their father, but as he explained Jubil's stance, they were soon convinced that it was best for everyone if the traitors were destroyed. It wasn't easy for any of them, but knowing the importance of their mission, they knew they had to keep their emotions contained. Besides, their apparently insane mother was, for all intent purposes, already dead. That was sufficient justification in their minds.

Immediately, Gary, his boys, and their troops set out across the land, taking no prisoners. They would find a group of believers, capture them, and then give them a chance to recant their belief in the King and pledge their allegiance to Jubil. They found very few that would do so, leaving them with no choice but to behead the believers and leave them for the animals to devour.

Every believer captured was interrogated to find out where his or her leaders were hiding.

None of them would give up any information, until finally one of them broke, "I'll give my allegiance to Jubil, please don't kill me!" pleaded the frightened Zera.

Gary held the sword to his throat. "Tell us where your leaders are, or you will die a painful death."

At that, the Zera cried out. "They are hiding out in the village of Zion, now please don't hurt me; I have a family."

Early the next morning, Gary and his troops mounted their horses and set out for Zion. It was the village farthest away from the prison, about a day's ride. Gary informed his soldiers that they would arrive at night and take the town by surprise. He made it very clear that not one of the townspeople was to survive. As the dreary night fell on the unsuspecting town of Zion, Gary and his soldiers positioned themselves in the woods. They watched quietly, and when the last lantern was doused, Gary gave the command.

Swiftly, the troops rode furiously down the hill into the village. Without warning, they set houses on fire and watched the occupants clamor out of them. As they came running out, the soldiers slaughtered them by the dozens. No one in Zion was prepared. The adults and children alike were ambushed as they fled from their houses. Not one was spared. The soldiers had no mercy.

Throughout the valley, as the massacre raged on, the sounds of screams and cries could be heard coming from the village. No one could help them. Finally, Gary came upon the house where Karen and the other leaders resided. The soldiers had already set the house on fire and killed those trying to escape from the front. Gary saw Karen through the window heading toward the back of the house. He had not expected anyone to try and escape through the rear since that was where the fire was burning the most intense. Karen jumped through the back door and fell to the ground where she rolled to put out the flames that threatened her life. When she stopped, she looked up to see Gary standing over her with his sword pointed down at her chest.

REMEMBER

Karen pleaded with him. "What are you doing, Gary? Are you so blind?"

"You are the one who is blind," said Gary, trembling.

Karen looked deep into his eyes. "Will you kill your own wife? Don't you know that I still love you, Gary. Has Jubil so deceived you that you would kill your own children's mother?"

Sweat began to appear on Gary's forehead. "Be quiet; if they were here right now they would kill you themselves because of all the harm you've caused. People are dying because of you!"

"Gary, it's not me who is killing; you are the one with the sword!"

"We have to kill your kind to save the rest of us," said Gary in self-defense. "It's because of all the trouble you and your followers are causing—and for what? Believing in a fairy tale and a false king?"

"He is not a false king," said Karen, now shedding a tear. "Don't you remember what He did for us and how we used to live in peace? Look around you, can't you remember color? Look at me; look at my color!"

Gary looked down at Karen and saw something that he had so long forgotten. It was the eyes of someone filled with love. Gary lowered his sword and turned around, wiping a tear from his eye. Karen stood up. As she turned to go to him, one of Gary's troops came running up from behind her and stabbed her through her heart. Petrified, she looked down at the tip of the sword.

Gary, watching what took place, screamed, "You fool! What have you done?"

"I'm doing what you ordered me to do, sir," said the trooper, pulling his sword from her body.

As Karen dropped to the ground, Gary grabbed her in his arms, pulled her tight to his chest, weeping intensely.

"I'm so sorry, Karen," said Gary. "So sorry."

"I forgive you, Gary," said Karen, in a soft voice. "Remember, I love you, Gary, and if this is what it takes for you to see the truth, I will gladly die for you."

It was when she had finished speaking that Karen drew her last breath.

Gary jumped to his feet, wiped his tears, and cried out in anger, "Nooooo!"

Gary could not remember the King, or what exactly it was that Karen believed in, but he did remember that he once loved her. His mind was racing, not knowing whom to blame, when at once he came to the conclusion that whoever caused her to believe all this nonsense in the first place had to be held accountable. Instantly, Gary was filled with bitterness and rage. Instead of being angry at himself or Jubil, he was angry with the King and His believers. More than ever, Gary believed in what he was doing, and knew that to complete his mission, he was going to have to harden his heart even more. He vowed to destroy every remaining believer if it was the last thing he did.

Jubil couldn't have been happier!

A BIG MISTAKE

Karen's words haunted Gary for days. The look on her face that night was forever etched in his mind. Time had passed, and though he had questions, Gary continued toward his goal. His calling card had been left throughout the cities of the garden. It was a common occurrence to see a dead, rotting corpse of a believer hung from a fence or a tree, displayed as a warning to all.

Fear was an effective tactic; nobody wanted to be a believer under those conditions. At least they didn't want to advertise it, if they were. Still, in secret places, the Zera were found gathered together, reading and speaking about the King. This was a constant source of frustration for Gary and his cohorts. How could these believers keep popping up?

"They are dying for their faith," cried a disillusioned Gary, as he was taking a walk with Luke and Jake. "What is their motivation? Why would they want to follow someone who is not real?"

"Because he is real," came a voice out of the shadows.

"What?" queried Gary. "Who goes there?"

Luke and Jake drew their swords. Gary turned to see who it was, but could only see what seemed to be the glowing red eyes of a viper. He was startled when Jubil stepped out of the darkness, clothed in all of his splendor. He had been listening to Gary talking to his sons and figured that they needed to be informed of a truth. Gary and his sons awaited Jubil's explanation, confused by what they had seen in the darkness.

"The King they read about in the *Book* is not fictional; He is real!" said Jubil.

A BIG MISTAKE

"What are you saying?" asked Luke.

"Hear me out." Continued Jubil. "It is true; He is our creator and King. The problem is that this King is not this wonderful King who is described in that *Book*. When He wrote the *Book*, He distorted the truth. That's because He is a liar and a deceiver. I know firsthand."

Jubil was quite artful with his words, twisting the Zeras' thoughts, causing them to believe what he wanted them to about the King. How else could Jubil reveal his plan to attack the King if the Zera still thought He was only a myth? Reverting back to his original lie, Jubil poured it on thick.

"Gary, there's something I haven't told you about the King. It's true that many years ago He created all of you. He did have good intentions at first, but then He became afraid."

"Afraid of what?" asked Gary.

"Well, Gary, let me explain—you see, the King was afraid of what would happen if you came into maturity. When the King created you, He placed you here in the garden. He then called for me and my mighty Malachs to protect and watch over you. As you matured, the King noticed how strong you were becoming. Some of the Zera became disobedient. I wanted to work with them and give them a second chance, but the King was determined to terminate all of you. The Malachs and I took a stand on your behalf, and the King banished us to this horrible prison that was created for you. That is when we were given the name Rah Malachs. After that, He caused confusion to rise up in you to make you forget that any of it ever took place, but before you totally had forgotten, some of the Zera set us free. Together, we began freeing the others from His curse, but this caused the King to retaliate. He rewrote history, using lies, and put His version of the truth in that *Book* to draw the Zera back to Him. He wants to deceive all of you and use as many of you as He can to destroy me and the Rah Malachs. That is how it will be, unless you decide to stand with me."

"Of course, I will stand with you. I believe in what you are doing. What I don't understand is why anyone would die for some king they don't know and one they can't even see," said Gary.

"Because of the confusion he placed in them," said Jubil.

"How does He do it? Without coming here Himself, how do new believers keep appearing out of nowhere?" asked Gary.

"Because of the *Book*," responded Jubil, sounding frustrated.

"The *Book*?" asked Jake.

"Yes! *The Book of Remembrance*, the one I've been telling you about. Many of the others still have a copy of the *Book*. If we want to stop a tree from producing fruit, we don't keep plucking the apples, instead we destroy the tree at the root. We are plucking the apples by killing believers. We need to destroy the books and kill the root. All of the books!" shouted Jubil, making sure they got the message.

"That's it! You're right! We have to get rid of every *Book* in the garden. Not only will we help you destroy the books, one day we will help you destroy this evil King. This is His fault! Karen's death is His fault! I hate Him for what He's done." Gary looked perturbed.

His boys stood with their father in agreement.

Jubil, quite pleased with their decisions, grinned, showing affirmation on the outside, while inside, he knew he had deceived them.

The next day, Luke and Jake set out on their mission, searching for and destroying the books. They were very thorough, leaving no stone unturned in their quest. Some of the Zera gave up the books happily and watched them burn, while others fought to keep their books, whether they knew what was in the *Book* or not. Within one month, Luke and Jake had combed the entire garden, every village, and every house, and to their knowledge not a *Book* remained, or so they thought.

Billowy smoke rose from the towns throughout the garden as Luke and Jake headed home. Fiery, red piles of ashes were the only evidence that the books ever existed. They would sleep well tonight. Their father and Jubil would surely be proud of them.

A BIG MISTAKE

Upon arriving at the prison, Jubil met them at the gate.

"Come in," he said, congratulating them both. "Let's eat and drink to celebrate the success of your mission."

Luke and Jake proudly joined Jubil inside. The table was set with the choicest meats and finest wines, just like at the picnic. Candles dimly lit the dark, musty room. Gary was already seated along with the other Zera and Rah Malachs.

As they dined, Jubil picked up his old violin, and while playing pleasant music, said, "You have both done an outstanding job and deserve the highest praise." Jubil played and a mist filled the room.

The next morning, none of them had any recollection of the mission, or that the books ever existed.

Above the perforated veil, Gabriel had witnessed the destruction of the books. In haste, he flew back to the kingdom and reported what he saw. "My Lord, my Lord, it doesn't look good. Most of the believers are dead now, and Jubil has destroyed all of the books. I am sorry, King Adonai. Jubil seems to have outsmarted us. I believe Jubil has us in a stalemate, without any new believers, the veil can't be weakened any more."

The King responded, "Jubil was not quite as thorough as it would appear. In fact, there is one important detail that he missed."

"What is that?" asked Gabriel.

"Notice who he put in charge of destroying all the books," said the King.

Gabriel quickly answered, "Why, yes, he had Luke and Jake in charge. They, too, are very good at what they do."

"This is true." said the King. "But you failed to notice that when Luke and Jake cleaned the books out of the garden, two homes were missed!"

"Two?" said Gabriel, wondering whose houses they were.

"Yes," the King replied, "Jubil, in his overconfidence, forgot to have them start by cleaning out their own homes. Then, to top it off, he caused them to forget that the *Book* ever existed. That was a big mistake. This stalemate, as you call it, is about to end, leaving us on the winning side." The King was excited about the course of events, and hoped it gave the Malachs a sense of peace.

Back at the garden, Jubil approached Gary and his two sons, asking them to move into his headquarters (formerly known as the prison) with him. He wanted to keep a tighter reign on them so nothing would foil his plan. The three of them felt honored that Jubil had chosen them, not realizing his true motives. It was an unsuspected promotion for them.

"Go now," said Jubil. "Pack your things and move in at your leisure."

So off they went to gather their belongings. Luke arrived at his home first and began packing right away.

"Where should I start?" said Luke, looking at all the junk he had acquired. "I guess I need to start at the top and work my way down."

So up to the attic he went. As he was cleaning, he stumbled across an old book.

The King, watching, nudged Gabriel and pointed down to the garden. "Imagine that," he said.

Luke picked up the *Book* thinking that it looked familiar, but had no recollection of where he had gotten it. The cover was hard to read, so he blew off the dust and tried to wipe it clean.

Now able to make out the title, he read the words out loud, "*The Book of Remembrance*. Hmmm that's strange," he said. "I have a *Book of Remembrance* that I truly don't remember. This will be interesting," chuckling to himself.

Taking a break from his work, Luke took the *Book* and went to the kitchen to relax for a while. As he started reading, he found the story to be quite fascinating. It told about a magnificent kingdom, comprised of a beautiful city and palace where a King lived along with His servants, called Malachs, and animals. Everything was full of life, from the trees to the rocks. Most interesting, it seemed, was that the King had everything except a family.

Luke read on, more intrigued with each paragraph. When he came to the part where the King created the Zera, he saw how

A BIG MISTAKE

one of the King's Malachs became jealous and conspired against the King, causing one third of the Malachs to turn evil and follow him. He learned about the war that took place in the kingdom and saw how the Zera were moved to a garden paradise. The *Book* told how the evil Malachs were captured and locked away in a prison that was surprisingly close to the garden where the Zera lived. He thought that it all sounded like a nice fairy tale, but he began to read that there was disobedience in the garden, allowing the evil Malachs to be set free from the prison, filling the beautiful garden with darkness.

As he continued, the story seemed familiar, and an eerie feeling encompassed him, as if he was doing something wrong. Suddenly, he heard a knock on the door. He sat the book down and went to see who it was.

The person outside pounded impatiently. "Open up, it's the Rah Malachs," shouted a gravelly voice.

Luke hesitated for a moment, wondering what they could possibly want with him. Quickly hiding the *Book*, he unlatched the door. The door was thrown open with great force. Luke was startled, then surprised, to see that it was only his brother Jake joking around with him.

"Don't do that to me ever again!" Luke shouted angrily, yet still relieved that it was only his brother.

"Hey, don't get so uptight. Why are you so nervous, anyway?" Jake asked.

"Well, actually," said Luke, "I am packing my things, so I'm kind of busy right now."

"Busy? You don't look too busy!" said Jake.

"It may not look like it, but I am," said Luke. "Right now I'm looking at something."

"Well," Jake said, "I'm starving; how about if I fix myself a bite to eat?"

"Help yourself," said Luke.

Luke sat back down and continued reading the *Book*. He was mesmerized by it now; questions were stirring on the inside of him. The story seemed to be about him and his life in the garden. In fact, the evil Malach in the *Book* sounded a whole lot like Jubil. Luke was plodding through the *Book* when, suddenly he was taken by something very peculiar. He noticed that the two Zera twins were named Luke and Jake, just like he and his brother, and their parents had the same names, Gary and Karen. Slowly, Luke began to remember.

It was then that a strange light flickered off the page and caught Luke's eye. Immediately, he had a vision and started seeing images of himself and his brother doing the things described in the *Book*. At first he thought he was losing his mind as memories continued to surface. Another light sparked another memory—this one about how things used to be when the garden was perfect. He recalled how there used to be unity and peace among the Zera.

Closing the Book, he exclaimed, "Oh my goodness. It can't be."

Jake, setting down his sandwich asked, "What is it? What can't be?" He had no idea what was going to happen next.

"I remember!" said Luke.

"Remember what?" spouted Jake.

"I remember the King. I remember our King. It's all coming back to me now. Somehow, I remember His name. I can see His face and the kingdom where we once lived. It's all right here in this book I found."

Jake, confused by Luke's words, asked, "What book?"

Luke looked up, and holding out an old, dark, dusty book, replied, "This book; it's called *The Book of Remembrance*."

"Where did you find that old thing?" asked Jake.

"I found it up in the attic. I was up there cleaning and noticed it lying dusty and dirty tucked away in a corner, as if it was purposely placed there, and yet I don't remember owning it. I believe this book holds the answers to all of our questions."

Jake angrily interrupted. "What are you saying? You're talking crazy; how do you come up with this stuff?"

Luke looked at his brother. With a tear running down his face, he asked, "Jake, try to think back, how much can you remember about our past? Tell me, if you can, who are we? Where did we come from? Why are we here in the garden?"

Jake paused for a moment, stumped by Luke's questions.

"Well?" Luke asked.

"I don't know; I haven't ever given it much thought," said Jake.

"Don't you remember, Jake, a few years ago when we were in the backyard one evening lying on the ground, staring up at the stars, wondering what life was all about? We used to dream and talk about life being so much more than just living and dying. We knew there had to be something bigger than us out there, but look at us now. It's like we only believe in what we're programmed to believe, in what Jubil tells us to believe. Here lately we've been so busy and so preoccupied with serving Jubil that we have become calloused to the thought of something more. We mock all the believers because they believe by faith, and yet don't we believe the same way?"

Jake looked at Luke inquisitively, as Luke continued. "Think about it Jake. What foundation do we have for what we believe?"

"Again, Luke, I can't say that I've thought about it that much lately," responded Jake.

"I know, I was the same way until my eyes were opened just a few minutes ago. Up until then, like most Zera, I, too, was serving Jubil with no real direction in life, not knowing where I came from or where I was going. I have been following Jubil faithfully, and why? Could we have been blinded by his words? You have to listen to me Jake! I know the truth about Jubil and what he is up to. It's all in this *Book*."

Jake was still confused, and even a bit worried about his brother, yet he felt like part of what Luke was saying made sense. Jake knew that he had unanswered questions about life himself, but this seemed way too farfetched.

The only binding factor was that Jake had always looked up to Luke and was confident that his brother wouldn't be easily deceived. So, with some reservations, yet more curiosity, he said, "Show me this *Book*."

REMEMBER

Luke began reading to Jake, pointing out different writings in the *Book*. Every once in a while, Jake would grab the *Book* and say, "Let me see that," and then, after reading for himself, say, "How could this *Book* know so much about me?"

Jake read and read, and like a dissipating fog lifting from his mind, he gradually remembered all that had happened— including how Jubil had deceived them. He was devastated at the recollection of having killed anyone, let alone Zera that were once his friends. Suddenly, he remembered his mother. In agony, he fell to his knees, balling "Nooooo! How could it be? How could Jubil have deceived us so easily?"

Simultaneously, Luke fell on his knees, and both of them wept for some time. Now composed, they looked out in the direction of the sea and said, out loud, and with much conviction, "We believe you, King Adonai, and from this day forward we will do everything within our power to tell everyone about you!"

Two bright spheres of light penetrated the veil and fell upon Luke and Jake. Instantly, they were filled with color from head to toe. Both of them stood up, vowing before the King and each other to help as many as possible to believe. They had always thought their mother was crazy, now they knew the truth. She wasn't mad; she was right after all, and she was brave enough to make a stand for what she believed. Luke and Jake were humbled by the knowledge that their mother was faithful to the King to the end. Before this day they thought of themselves as valiant warriors, but today they knew that, like their mother, they had now truly become mighty warriors, serving the King of kings. Today was a day of commitment to fight like their mother to the end, even unto death, if necessary, to honor their true Father and King.

THE FINAL BATTLE

Luke and Jake couldn't sleep all night. All they could think about was how the Zera had been deceived and how their destiny would have turned out had they not remembered the King before that final day—the day when the King would return for them. So when morning dawned, they set out on their mission with no regard for their own lives. It would not be an easy mission, but they had to try. They started with those that were closest to them, sharing their experience of how they remembered the King, then showing each of them the *Book*.

Though the Zera were hardened at heart, and very leery at first, they still listened out of respect for who Luke and Jake were, especially since their words were empowered by the King. As they shared, many began to remember, and all who remembered, believed. What started out slowly was now spreading like wildfire once again. Every time another one would believe, another light would pierce the dark veil, weakening it a little more. The King knew the time was near, the end was at hand.

Back at the prison, Jubil, clueless to what was happening, had been gloating over the fact that he thought he had once again outsmarted the King. He had decided earlier that instead of waiting on the King to come to the garden, they would make their own surprise attack on the kingdom. He was giggling to himself, thinking about the King's face when he, the Rah Malachs, and all of the remaining Zera came bursting into His kingdom to destroy Him. Jubil knew that with complete unity among the Zera that even the King's Malachs could not defeat them.

REMEMBER

As he lay there daydreaming about all that he had planned, one of the Rah Malachs burst through his door. "Jubil!" he cried.

Jubil jumped up, startled. "What is it?"

"We have serious problems in the garden," said the Rah Malach.

"This had better be important."

"This is important! Early this morning, Jake and Luke somehow began believing in the King. Not only did they remember, now they are telling others. They are acting just like their mother did. Come outside and see for yourself!" screeched the Rah Malach.

At once Jubil jumped up and ran outside. He looked up at the dark sky and noticed lights falling from the kingdom. "The veil!" he said. "It's weakening! We must stop this! We cannot let the veil be destroyed!"

Jubil growled angrily. This was the second time that he was so close to victory, only to have the King somehow try and spoil it. "Call Gary; gather the troops." ordered Jubil. "The time is now. We must destroy these new believers, along with Luke and Jake. Then we will attack the King."

The Rah Malach acted quickly. After calling Gary and gathering all the troops, Jubil explained everything and how Luke and Jake were now the ultimate traitors.

Gary was furious. How could his two boys turn on their own father? "The King will pay for this, first my wife, and now my boys, what else can He steal from me?"

Word soon got back to the twins and the other believers. Realizing the inevitable, Luke and Jake told the believers to gather in the valley closest to the sea. From there, they knew they could see the assault from every direction. On their way, each of them collected any weapon they could find. Luke and Jake knew how their father thought, and knew he would waste no time in making an attack without warning. There was no way they could outrun the Rah Malachs, nor could they dodge the ones who could fly, so there was no sense in trying to escape. Their only hope was to unite and fight as one. With tensions building, the group of

THE FINAL BATTLE

believers huddled in the center of the valley, waiting for the attack to begin.

Back at the kingdom, Michael was preparing his troops. They gathered before the King's palace, ready for battle, each dressed in armor and mounted on their white horses. Gabriel and his messengers flew overhead, awaiting the command from the King. The King stepped out of the palace, dressed for the first time in His battle attire. His armor was shimmering silver, decorated and polished to the highest brilliancy, covering Him from head to toe. The armor had sharp spikes rising up from the shoulders, arms, and the backside of His gloves. One large spike came up from his helmet, with a tassel made from pure golden strands. A beautiful two-edged sword was sheathed to His side. The handle was made of pearl and precious jewels. The King removed His helmet to speak.

"Look at that," said one of the Malachs.

His hair was the whitest white, and a fire glowed from His eyes. As He drew His sword, so much power was released that it made the sound of loud rolling thunder. The Malachs stared in awe, then the King began to speak, and the ground trembled.

"The time is upon us," He began. "With one more believer, the veil will be weakened enough for us to attack."

"Lord, how is that ever going to happen?" asked Gabriel. "They are engaged in battle now; there is no time for them to make any new believers."

"Don't be afraid. My word is stronger than any sword. Believe me, it will not return to me void. It will accomplish all that I have sent it to do," replied the King.

In the valley, the war had already begun. Gary and all the nonbelieving Zera attacked from every side, just as Luke and Jake expected. The Rah Malachs ran quickly, attacking randomly from both the front and rear. Flying Rah Malachs watched from above for any opportunity to attack. In all reality, it appeared to be an easy win for Gary, but the strength that the believers obtained was greater than he anticipated.

REMEMBER

Suddenly, a slight trembling shook the ground, and everyone stopped and looked in the direction from which it came. There was Jubil coming over the hill, mounted on his evil black steed. As he topped the peak, his horse stomped and snorted loudly, his nostrils flared and his bloodshot eyes bulged from his head. He was chomping at the bit; the smell of blood and the sound of clashing swords made him anxious for battle. Jubil was wearing dark armor, which was not only his trademark, but also represented the condition of his soul. From his side, he drew a sword that appeared to be on fire. His glowing red eyes peered through his dark helmet, making his eyes and sword the only color around him. It created a striking contrast to the darkness now enveloping the scene.

Jubil shouted, "The victory will be mine!" Then his horse reared up, snorting and blowing smoke from its nostrils.

At the bottom of the valley, the fighting continued in full force. Jubil gave his horse a kick, and then charged down the hill, plunging straight into the believers. He was fiercely slaying them left and right with his sword. The Rah Malachs who were flying drew their bows and began shooting flaming arrows. Believers were dropping like flies, and it looked as if the battle would soon be over, but the remaining believers pulled tighter together and continued to fight.

Jubil called out to Gary, "Split their ranks. We have to split them up. You and I need to plow through the middle of them and force them to separate."

"Yes, sir!" shouted Gary.

Jubil and Gary met side by side and continued slaying believers. They were very powerful warriors, and few could stand against them. Some tried to fight back, but many fell by their swords. As Jubil and Gary pushed their way through the crowd, the believers were forced to spread out. Once they were divided, their power began to weaken, and many more perished.

In the kingdom, the Malach's horses reared up and pawed the ground as well. It took all the Malachs's strength to hold them back, as they awaited the King's signal.

THE FINAL BATTLE

The battle was raging. Jubil again shouted over to Gary, "We need to destroy the leaders, then the rest will scatter!"

Gary looked through the crowd, saying angrily, "There they are over there; let's kill them!"

Jubil let out a wicked laugh, kicked his horse and rode forcefully straight toward Luke and Jake, killing any believer that got in his way. At the same time, Luke and Jake were engaged in heavy combat with both the Rah Malachs and the nonbelievers and did not notice Jubil coming.

Jubil came from behind with Gary following. One of the believers cried out to warn the two brothers, but it was too late. Before they could turn to see what the danger was, Jubil struck them both with his mighty sword. The power of his sword cut clean through their armor, knocking them both to the ground. They were badly hurt, yet tried to roll over and continue the fight. Before they could move, though, both Jubil and Gary were on them, holding them down with their feet, pressing on each of their throats.

Gary, cried out, "How could you have turned on Jubil and your own father?"

Gary stood over Jake, breathing hard, anger permeating from his very being. He raised his sword about to thrust it down into Jake's chest when Luke cried out, "Father, before you kill us, just let us say one thing in our defense."

"What is it, you traitor?" shouted Gary.

Luke tried to speak, "The King—"

But before he could say another word, Jubil slammed his sword down into Luke's throat, saying viciously, "No, don't listen to him."

Gary was still looking at Jubil when Jake erupted, "King Adonai wants you to know that He created you and He loves you."

Gary turned around in a fit of anger and raised his sword to kill Jake.

Jubil yelled, "Quickly, kill him, kill him you fool!"

At that, Gary took a double take at Jubil, as if wondering why he was in such a hurry. *What threat could Jake pose now?* he thought to himself.

REMEMBER

Jake took advantage of that moment and said sympathetically, "King Adonai wants you to remember, father, remember!"

Gary turned this time, not hesitating to kill Jake.

He raised his sword, and again Jake shouted, "Father, remember!"

"Remember! Ha!" said Gary as the sword was coming down.

"Remember! Remember!" Gary murmured, when suddenly he stopped with his sword one inch from Jake's chest.

"Remember?" said Gary in a confused state. "Remember King Adonai? King Adonai?"

"Nooo!" screamed Jubil. "Kill him now, kill him, kill him!"

Jubil tried to run at Gary to stab him in the back, but now the believers jumped on him, holding him back and slowing him down.

Jake lay there, looking up at his father, crying, "Remember, father; it's not too late."

Gary didn't know what was going on inside of him. Confused, he turned to look at Jubil and instantly noticed the red burning eyes piercing the darkness, reminding him of what he had seen earlier in the shadows. He turned back to Jake and looked into his eyes. When he did, he saw the same love he had seen in his wife's eyes. Suddenly, Jake's eyes sparkled, and Gary drew back.

"What was that?" Gary muttered. He paused and then began repeating the word, *remember*, over and over, until finally, images started flashing before his eyes. The first image was the garden as it once was with the waterfall, stream, animals, and the villages that had been built. Then he envisioned the King and the Malachs visiting them in the garden. All of a sudden, he saw the kingdom and the King sitting on His throne in all His glory. The onslaught of memories overwhelmed him now, and, in his mind's eye, he could clearly remember the day when Jubil first began deceiving him. Staggering, Gary dropped his sword and looked at the blood on his hands.

Jake said to him, "Everything will be all right, father, we forgive you. The King forgives you, and you know mother forgives you."

Gary had a look of terror mixed with grief on his face. He held his head in his hands, shaking and weeping uncontrollably. "What have I done?" said Gary. "What have I done? How could I have turned my back on the King? Oh, Karen, Luke, Jake— how can you ever forgive me?"

Meanwhile, Jubil had been killing the Zera that were trying to hold him down. Seeing this, Gary jumped up; grabbed his sword, and helped Jake to his feet.

Then he hollered at the top of his lungs, "Jubil, your fight is with me now!"

Jubil turned and looked at Gary, smiling wickedly. Just then a bright light crashed through the veil and blasted into Gary's chest.

Jubil watched with fear as Gary raised his sword and shouted, "Fight for the King!"

Color was covering his body as he ran toward Jubil. Jubil spread his wings and flew up into the sky in revolt.

"Now what will you do? You know you're no match for me. Give up and I'll have mercy on you." Jubil pitched his bluff trying to intimidate Gary and the remaining believers.

Suddenly, the sound of his boasting was silenced by a loud rumbling noise coming from the eastern sky. It sounded like many stampeding horses accompanied by thunder and lightning. The ground shook so violently that it was hard to stand, and the fighting ceased. Every eye was fixed on the sky above the sea. Suddenly, a loud trumpet sounded and the dark veil burst wide open, splitting from top to bottom. When it did, light flashed across the sky. The veil was now split from end to end, and, in a blink of an eye, the sky cleared. Clouds diminished and a pretty blue color took their place. Everyone's eyes were still adjusting to the great light when the shape of a large Zera, made of an even brighter light and riding on horseback, began to form off in the distance. Many other riders were appearing behind him. As they rode, color spread out across the land, leading their way like a red carpet entry.

Everything was beautiful in the eyes of the believers, but to Jubil and his followers, it was the embodiment of their doom and defeat. They let out a shriek and tried to flee.

Instantly, Luke and the bodies of other dead believers, nonbelievers, and Rah Malachs all disappeared.

Jake looked down to the spot where his brother had been lying and called out, "Luke!"

Then he looked to the sky, wondering what had just happened. He watched as the King rode on the wind, chasing Jubil.

Before Jake could look any further, Gary shouted to him, "Look, Jake, look!"

Jake turned his eyes up to see the King, and a great smile covered his face as he noticed, accompanying the King was Michael and Gabriel close behind Him. Then his smile grew larger for behind them, riding along side the other Malachs, were Aaron, Eden, Ryan, and Jared and—to his great surprise—there was his mother. He couldn't believe his eyes. All the believers that had died before him, many lives he was responsible for taking, were alive and well, riding with the King. A tear welled up in his eye, partly from joy, and partly from shame for what he had done in his past. He went to his knees and covered his face, but then one of the horsemen skidded to a stop right in front of him. When he looked up, he was filled with joy. There was his brother, Luke, stronger and more alive than ever. He had a glow around him like that of the King in all His glory.

Before he could say a word, Luke said, "Well, are you just going to sit there whimpering or are we going to see the end of this battle?"

Behind Luke was a beautiful white horse bowed down with one leg stretched forward. Jake looked at Luke, smiled, and mounted the horse. When he did, his body changed. He too glowed like the King. The horse stood up proudly, and they found their place in the King's army. Each believer mounted the horse that had been brought for them and joined the troops who were shining bright like the sun. Karen rode up to Gary and presented him with his new horse.

She looked down at Gary, and said, smiling, "The King said we would be together again some day, if I only believed. Welcome home, Gary."

All guilt left Gary as he walked up to Karen's horse and reached up to hug her. Karen leaped off the horse into Gary's arms, and they held each other for a moment before mounting their steeds. As they did, Gary shone like Karen and the rest of them. The Malachs now witnessed the power that had always been hidden within the Zera.

As the King advanced, light shot out of His sword and struck each of Jubil's followers. Jubil tried frantically to escape. The King pointed His sword at him, and while pronouncing his judgment, knocked him to the ground with a flash of light.

The King dismounted and walked up to Jubil; putting His foot on Jubil's chest, He held the sword to his throat, looked down at Jubil, and said, "Say it."

Jubil looked up and very reluctantly said in a quiet voice, "You are King."

"Say it so all can hear you," said the King, this time more aggressively.

Then Jubil said in a loud voice, "Yes, Lord, you are the King of all kings."

At that, the King turned to the Zera and said, "Bind Jubil and his followers in chains and follow me."

After they were bound securely, the Zera and Malachs followed the King to the prison. When they arrived, Jubil and each one of his followers, both Rah Malachs and Zera alike, were taken inside and locked up. That was when they noticed all of Jubil's followers that had died before and during battle were already there locked in chains. Fear and misery filled the eyes of the vanquished. Each was incarcerated in his own cell and separated from all the others, left to spend eternity totally alone. When they were finished locking up the Rah Malachs and non-believing Zera, the King and Zera, along with the Malachs, gathered outside. The King spoke, and the prison began to fold from side to side into a perfect box, and then it rose up and shot out into utter darkness, never to be seen or heard of again.

The King turned to all who were standing there and said to His Malachs, "Now you see. These who stand before you, they have overcome; they are my true children. They loved me because I first loved them. Because of their love, they found me when I could not be seen. This is what it was all about. If they could love me in darkness, then surely they will love me in light. Each one that you see standing before you has passed this test." The King triumphantly said, "Well done, my faithful ones! Well done indeed!" Then He turned back toward the kingdom and said, "Mount up, we are going home."

At the King's command, everyone mounted their horse, and cheered great shouts of joyful acclamation. They returned to the kingdom where everything good awaited them. Each of them saw their own mansion where they would live, and they fully recalled everything about their former life, whether they were born in the garden, or created in the kingdom. At the palace, the King had prepared a great feast for them. So, with great excitement, they gathered to eat and celebrate, both Zera and Malachs alike. There, in the radiant kingdom across the sea, they lived for all eternity with their great, merciful Father and King!

> All the ends of the Earth will remember and turn to the Lord.
>
> Psalm 22:27, NIV

e|LIVE

listen|imagine|view|experience

AUDIO BOOK DOWNLOAD INCLUDED WITH THIS BOOK!

In your hands you hold a complete digital entertainment package. In addition to the paper version, you receive a free download of the audio version of this book. Simply use the code listed below when visiting our website. Once downloaded to your computer, you can listen to the book through your computer's speakers, burn it to an audio CD or save the file to your portable music device (such as Apple's popular iPod) and listen on the go!

How to get your free audio book digital download:

1. Visit www.tatepublishing.com and click on the elLIVE logo on the home page.
2. Enter the following coupon code: 21e9-7dc1-c8a0-729c-e7c2-b679-b213-4d78
3. Download the audio book from your elLIVE digital locker and begin enjoying your new digital entertainment package today!